TRIASSIC PLANET

MICHAEL COLE

SEVERED PRESS
HOBART TASMANIA

TRIASSIC PLANET

Copyright © 2020 Michael Cole

WWW.SEVEREDPRESS.COM

ISBN: 978-1-922323-68-2

CHAPTER 1

Borrus wiped his arm over his forehead, his green sleeve turning dark from absorbing the sweat that accumulated. Malek was a hot planet. By Oh-ten-hundred hours, it was ninety degrees. By noon, it was a hundred. The only reason he wore long sleeves was to protect against the annoying little mosquitos that buzzed around him. A single bite would leave an itchy welt that would last for weeks.

There were a dozen of the little bloodsuckers zipping around his head. The buzzing of their wings was enough to drive a man crazy. More than once, Borrus was tempted to blast his shotgun into the little horde. Maybe that would teach the bastards to keep away.

He felt a sting on the lobe of his left ear.

"Bastard prick bug!" he snapped, slapping his palm to his head. He looked at his hand, seeing the squashed remains of the mosquito bathed in the blood it had drained from him. "Hope that tasted good."

"Got a problem there, Borrus?" He looked back at his fellow pirates, Regal and Candor. Both of them were smiling at their comrade's misfortune. As usual, the mosquitos seemed to steer clear of them. What boggled Borrus' mind was that these men wore sleeveless tactical vests, leaving plenty of space for the bugs to attack. Yet, they favored him, as though they knew they were being annoying. Candor took glee in this, hence that shit-eating grin that peered from behind that black goatee.

"It's this planet. It's got it in for me," Borrus said. They stopped and gazed at the jungle that surrounded them. Their view stopped at fifteen feet in any direction. Leaves as large as dinner plates hung from enormous branches. The size of these trees was an indication of how little mankind had visited this planet. Some of them stretched to nearly three hundred feet high, and were probably thousands of years old. Some had trunks as wide as Jeeps and the ground between them was layered with different kinds of flora. It was pleasant on the eyes, but not the body.

Patrolling around Mt. Dragoon was the most unfavorable of duties in this pirate settlement. Borrus even argued about disregarding it entirely. They had already killed any dangerous wildlife…all except those damned mosquitos! All that did was anger the pirate leader, Gillion, who demanded Borrus spend the rest of his time on Malek performing the patrol duty. It was a display of power and an effective one too. Borrus already knew that he had two choices: comply and deal with the misery, or refuse and be executed in a hail of gunfire. He recalled that conversation very well. With the dozen assault rifles already pointed at him, it was an easy decision.

"When will Gillion bring the physicist?" he asked.

"Maybe in another day or so," Regal said. "Gatton's forcing the prisoners to fix the last container over at Northwood."

Ah, Northwood, Borrus thought. It was somewhere he'd prefer to be. The ground was much more level than here. The forest was still thick but not to the point of blinding a man. Of course, they had trimmed it out, which helped. Too bad they couldn't get the trimmers over here to make his life a little easier.

"Come on. Let's get moving again," Candor said. He held his rifle with one hand and propped it back over his shoulder. "We only have a mile and a half to go. In thirty minutes, we'll be back at the dig site. Let's get there and have some food and water…and ointment for Borrus."

"I appreciate you thinking of me, boss," Borrus quipped.

"My knees could use the break," Regal said.

"Mine too, so let's go," Candor said.

****

The next half-mile took them through a maze of forest. Golden rays of sunlight poured down in little streams which reflected off the enormous green leaves as though they were mirrors. The plant life was almost lime-green in color, even in the bushes and low-hanging branches that struggled for any sunlight.

The ground was at a twelve degree angle. Uneven to begin with, it made walking strenuous, even for someone as conditioned as Candor. He was eager to move up in the ranks, so he didn't complain; at least, not to any superiors. But in his mind, he was screaming from boredom, aching joints, and blisters on his feet.

He focused on the bird calls that echoed deep in the forest. He could hear small branches cracking as small primates clamored over each other for small berries that grew at the high reaches of the canopy. He wasn't an outdoorsman and had no problem shooting some of these animals for nothing else other than target practice, but he did appreciate the background noise they provided during these patrols. He could hear the little monkeys squirming about somewhere high above.

Maybe they're getting it on, he thought. He smiled at his unspoken joke.

A sharp crack echoed through the forest. All the casual sounds of the forest turned to alarmed animals fleeing. Birds took to the skies, while the monkeys and critters scurried for their dens.

The trio stopped. Another series of cracks popped off rapidly. Each of them had been around firearms long enough to recognize the sound of rifle fire.

"What the hell's going on?" Borrus said. He had his shotgun pressed to his shoulder, partially raised. He watched the forest but saw nothing but trees.

"Maybe someone's out hunting?" Regal suggested.

"You don't hunt with your rifle on full auto," Borrus reminded him.

More sounds. Engines roared in the distance, followed by sounds of tires slicing through forest ground. A few moments passed before the patrollers realized there were multiple vehicles driving from the campsite. And they weren't coasting—these vehicles were all going at high speed, through thick forest.

"Perhaps the prisoners staged a riot," Regal said, cautiously. Candor shook his head. No way the hostages could overtake the pirates, who were all armed with automatic weapons. Something else was going on.

Candor activated his commlink.

"Orbiter to Starlight? What's your status?" There was no answer. Several more gunshots rang out in rapid succession. It stopped suddenly, and a man's scream took its place.

Borrus' shotgun was now level. "Let's go! It's coming from that way!" He pointed ahead with the muzzle. The man screamed again briefly, stopping abruptly. There were sounds of a struggle, followed by a second burst of rifle fire. It too ceased suddenly as another scream echoed through the forest.

"Go!" Candor ordered. The three men took flanking positions and rushed through the forest. They kept a distance of three meters, enough to keep within sight of each other. They raced through the forest, weaving between trees and bushes.

By now the forest had gone silent. Candor held up a fist, signaling to the others to halt. They crouched low, weapons pointed ahead. Candor extended a finger, pointing to a rifle in the dirt several meters ahead. Its grip and barrel were stained with fresh blood. Borrus, who was on the right, watched the trees intently. Though he couldn't see anything, he could sense he was being watched.

"Move up," Candor ordered.

"Candor, wait," Borrus said.

"I said…move up." Those last two words were spoken through a tense scowl. He stood to a half-crouch and moved toward the rifle. To his left, Regal moved parallel with him. Borrus hesitated briefly before following. He kept his eyes on the trees. Every ripple of the leaves tempted him to squeeze the trigger. Finally, he looked down to examine the rifle.

The magazine was two-thirds spent. There were small grooves along the top of the barrel. They were narrow, as though someone had wacked it several times with an axe. Beyond the rifle was a trail of blood that had been smeared over some flattened brush.

They followed the trail for a hundred feet, only to come to a large puddle of blood and guts. Scattered over the ground were shreds of clothing and small strips of flesh, as though the pirate had been put through a blender with no lid.

Candor tried the commlink again. "This is Orbiter. Is anyone out there? Respond. Respond, damn you! We have hostiles out here." There was no response. He started to broaden the range to reach out to one of the settlements.

"Candor, I recommend we head back to camp," Borrus said. "There's fewer trees, better line of sight…we'll stand a better chance."

The pirate thought for a moment, then nodded.

Before he could speak, the bushes exploded behind them. They turned, seeing a maze of black claws swinging down over Regal. The pirate screamed as his flesh was torn. The creature stood upright, its brown tail thrashing back and forth as though propelling it into him. Its triangular head gaped open in a lightning fast motion, baring triangular teeth, which closed down over his neck. Three-fingered claws drove between his ribs. Then, as fast as it appeared, it turned back and disappeared into the forest with Regal in tow.

Borrus and Candor discharged their weapons, trying to aim in the path of… whatever that was. Their projectiles shredded bark and leaves. The two pirates ceased fire, then looked at each other, both wondering if they had hit the strange beast.

"Let's go after it," Candor said.

"What the hell *was* it?!" Borrus shouted.

"I don't know, but it got Regal!" Candor loaded a fresh magazine and darted in the direction the creature went. He heard leaves exploding behind him and an ear-piercing shriek. He turned around in time to see the blur of leathery brown flesh and black claws descending on Borrus. It had jumped him from behind and drove him face-first into the dirt. The creature was eleven feet from the tip of its nose to that of its tail. Its reptilian jaws contained over forty inch-and-a-half-long teeth. On each foot was an eight-inch crescent-shaped claw. Razor-sharp, one of them punctured Borrus' back directly between the shoulders. He let out a scream, flailing his arms and legs.

Candor had a split second to react. Though the creature had its claw buried in his comrade, its yellow eyes were on him. He already had an idea of how fast it was. By the time he could position his weapon, it would already be on top of him. Best option was to run and hope it would be too preoccupied to give chase.

Candor broke into the fastest sprint he had ever run. In seconds, he put over a hundred yards between him and the creature. Judging by the agonizing screams of the man he abandoned, the creature had chosen to remain. Candor forced it from his mind and kept moving. He stumbled twice over the rough terrain, both times barely managing to regain his footing.

There were footsteps moving alongside him. Heavy ones, getting nearer and nearer. In his peripheral vision was a blur of motion. Candor yelled and turned to the left, spraying bullets wildly. The thing had already darted away and disappeared into the trees. Candor didn't stop. He swung the muzzle back and forth, sending bullets soaring through the forest until, finally, the rapid cracks were replaced by silence. He squeezed the trigger again and again, hearing the dull clicks of an empty firearm. After several attempts, his senses returned to him and he ejected the empty mag and reached for a new one.

The empty mag bounced off the ground and settled in a pool of sunlight. Candor pressed a fresh one into his rifle. Suddenly, he noticed that the sunlight had disappeared, overtaken by a large angular shadow. He could feel hot breath against his neck and heard the crinkling of fallen leaves as it crouched slightly, ready to spring.

Frozen with tension, he turned his head slightly and looked back. It was right there, staring at him with yellow eyes. Hot breath escaped its slightly agape jaws. Its arms were coiled back against its chest, ready to lash out. It held this pose for what seemed like an eternity. It was like it wanted its prey to know what was coming.

Candor's breathing quickened and his heart thumped so hard it felt as though it would burst through his chest. The tension released with a mad scream, and the pirate spun on his heel. A high-energy force struck. All of a sudden, he was on the ground, his weapon flinging behind a wall of brush behind him. All he saw next was a blur of motion.

Black daggers sank into his chest and pulled his torso apart like tissue paper. Jaws clamped down on his arm then shook, slicing skin and muscle and snapping the bone. The claws pulled further then raked down, snapping several rips and exposing his lungs.

Another pair of teeth found his leg. More claws entered his stomach, ripping the entrails free. Meats came out in bloody strands. The forest had come alive with these reptilians, who gathered around the fresh kill and bit at anything they could sink their teeth into. Many focused on his belly while others tugged on his legs and arms. They stripped his flesh like a school of piranhas. Before the sweet release of death, Candor felt tension on all four limbs at once. Like a medieval prisoner being drawn and quartered, his body split into pieces.

After a few minutes, the creatures scattered, leaving nothing but bone lying in blood-soaked dirt.

CHAPTER 2

In the black of space, Malek's green surface was nearly as bright as the star that gave it life. The planet was covered in lush green, with the exception of a few lakes and its arctic polar regions. Discovered two standard years ago, Malek was equal to Earth's size. Its atmosphere had been cleared by the Galactic Center for Disease Control as non-toxic, allowing geologists and surveyors to conduct further inspections of the planet.

Staff Sergeant Akira Sakai gazed at the planet through the viewing window. For a brief moment, he allowed himself to be mesmerized by the clarity of its atmosphere and verdant surface. With his fascination came sadness and frustration. He knew what the next few years would bring to this planet. Contractors would be hired by the government to ship logging and digging equipment to start plundering resources. It was the way of the universe, he supposed. Perhaps the companies would actually take the time to plant new seedlings in place of the trees they cut this time. His mind flashed to a memory on a similar planet known as Rominse, which had turned into a giant dustbowl after its resources had been stripped clean.

The memory sparked a small cough, the last remnant of the dirt that filled his lungs during his stay on Rominse. The logging companies had stripped the land, and with nothing left to hold it down, the dirt kicked up with each breeze. Sakai spent the next few months coughing it out. He remembered looking upon an ocean of black desert that had been green just a couple years prior. Sakai understood the human race was expanding into space, and to survive, resources were needed. The problem was that the companies weren't doing it responsibly and the damned United World

Order did nothing to maintain the stability of the ecosystems they harvested from. And here they were at the next stop.

Sakai gave one last gaze at the planet, then snapped his mind into focus. He was here on a mission, not to gawk at pretty sights. He turned around to the interior of the armory. Three of his squad were there gearing up, bantering back and forth as they always did, on duty and off.

"Do I really have to wear this thing, Sarge?" Shawn Ward held his helmet then cocked his head, flaunting his thinly trimmed mohawk. On each side of his skull were laser burns, a reminder of a narrow escape from hostile forces on the desert planet of Tanegra. The heat felt as though it were returning with that burning gaze from the Staff Sergeant. "I guess so." He pressed the helmet down over his hair and clipped it shut.

"Not going down there with a damn parakeet," Sakai said, sparking laughter from the other two troops.

"Too bad there's nothing to cover his face," Ryan Pharris said.

"Oh, you're one to talk, *Pinky*," Ward shot back, pointing at Pharris' left hand. There lay the source of his nickname. Three years prior, he had been providing sniper fire during the occupation when an enemy sniper round grazed his hand, severing his pinky right at the knuckle. Luckily, he had seen the muzzle flash and was able to extract revenge on the dirtbag. The nickname caught on almost immediately.

Pinky looked at his hand, then back at his fellow soldier. "You're seriously comparing my hand to your face?" He pointed at the third soldier in the room, Mike Landon. "Hell! His face even outranks yours. Isn't that right there, Mr. *State Trooper*?!?"

"Oh, here we go again," Landon said, brushing a finger over his bushy mustache. He finished loading his rifle and turned around to glare at his companions, braced for the incoming volley of jokes about how he looked like a hillbilly cop. Well, it seemed to fit with this trio. He looked like a cop and Ward looked like a drug dealer with those scars and that hairdo. "Come on, I'm waiting," he said.

"Finish up," Sakai interrupted. "Once you're done, head to Briefing. I'll be there in three." Landon was the first one heading to the door.

"Thanks for sparing me, Sarge," he said. Pinky and Ward suddenly rushed the exit after him.

"What's your hurry, Landon? Is it National Donut Day?" Ward cackled.

"Oh, here we go," Landon moaned. Their voices faded into the corridor as Sakai clipped his standard ballistic armor over his combat fatigues. Designed to balance comfort and buoyancy with optimum protection, it consisted of a sandwich of materials molded to form a rigid shell that could deflect a standard five-five-six rifle-round. Like the combat fatigues, the armor was camouflage colored to help blend in with the forest surroundings. He strapped on his matching shin-guards then headed for the rifle rack.

He plucked a Vanquisher-Riptide rifle from the slot and began his inspection. The Vanquisher-Riptide, VR for short, was constructed with lightweight heat-resistant aluminide alloy with a carbon steel outer casing which added appropriate weight to the weapon. Like most military rifles that came before it, the VR was capable of firing semi-auto, three-round bursts, and fully automatic fire. The model he selected was a VR-13, which contained a lever-action grenade launcher on its under-barrel. Other models, such as VR-11, contained a flamethrower with an eight-ounce fuel cannister. On the weapon's upper receiver was an LED flasher. Green meant the weapon was fully loaded, orange was for half a mag, and ultimately it would blink red once the magazine reached its final ten rounds.

Sakai loaded an eighty-round magazine into the weapon and slapped it on the bottom to ensure it was fully latched. He attached as many additional magazines to the side-pockets of his body armor as possible. Next, he inspected his favorite Ice-Eagle sidearm before loading it with a magazine containing ten fifty-caliber bullets. Its six-inch barrel poked through the end of its holster, the silver tip standing out slightly against his camouflage. He packed some hand-grenades, a pair of thermal binoculars, and a double-edge knife. With his helmet in hand, he marched out into the briefing room.

His boots clunked against the metal floor. Walking always felt weird in space. Despite the advances in artificial gravity, it just never felt right for some reason. Though he moved normally, he always felt as though he was floating.

The team had assembled in the briefing room. In the center was a table containing a holographic display. Sakai moved to the left and gave his team a brief glance to make sure everyone was present. Ward, Pinky, and Landon were huddled on the far side of the table. Judging by Landon's cross expression, he had endured some more cop jokes. The others lined up opposite their Staff Sergeant.

On the left corner was Vance. Her arms protruded through a sleeveless vest, revealing skin so pale it looked as though she lived in the Arctic. No matter how many times she got sunburnt, it seemed she could never tan. In addition, her eyes were as blue as crystal. That, along with her Russian accent, landed her a few comedic comparisons with Siberian huskies from her teammates.

Next to her was Calloway. He was as far of a contrast from her as one could possibly get. His skin was so tan, he often looked as though he bathed near the surface of the sun. Part of growing up as a corn-fed farm boy from Georgia. And that corn stuck with him. Though by no means obese, he was the stockiest member of the group. Stocky, but strong as an ox…and as angry as a bear when the time was right.

A whole head shorter than him was Cutler, the team medic. A slight germaphobe, he was sanitizing his hands for the third time in a row.

"You know, Doc, people who do that are the ones who get sick all the time," Calloway spoke in a thick country accent.

"Yeah, fine," Cutler said. "I'll just let these hands get nice and greasy for the occasion where I'll have to dig a bullet out of your fat gut."

"I'm not sure you'll find anything but jerky in there," Hood said. The advanced weapons specialist smirked at his own joke and polished the barrel of his five-shot grenade launcher.

"Hey, before you finish practicing for your nightly routine, get that bag off the table," Sakai said, sparking laughter from the other soldiers. Hood, being a good sport, bared a toothy smile then yanked the nylon bag containing the heavy machine-gun and its mount. It hit the floor hard, causing his backup submachine-gun to sway at his left shoulder.

Sakai noticed something was off. Someone wasn't here.

"Why isn't everyone present? Fucking—Private Bodales! Report!" he shouted. His lax expression became one of fire and brimstone. Suddenly the atmosphere in the room was full of tension. "Where the hell is she?" he barked at the squad.

"Last I saw her, sir, was at the comm bay," Calloway answered.

"I told her to report," Vance said. "I guess she got caught up in—"

"I'll take care of it," Sakai said. He moved around the table with long strides and approached the starboard exit, knocking it open with an open palm before disappearing into the corridor.

****

Private Morgan Bordales withheld tears as she typed frantically at the computer. She could hear the pounding footsteps down the corridor behind her. She knew it was Sakai, but it didn't matter. She had to get the message out. She had checked the message receiver a dozen times since they came out of hyperspace. Not one message from the boy she hadn't seen in years, despite the hundreds she had written to him.

She tapped her fingers to the keyboard, her frantic motions littering the message with typos. *I really miss you. I haven't heard from you in months. Please message Mommy back if you can.* Backspace. Too desperate, even for a six-year old.

The door swung open with a loud crack. Morgan stood up in position of attention. Sakai gazed at her from top to bottom. Her red hair was unkempt and hanging at shoulder length. She had not collected her helmet or weapon yet. Her fatigues were full of wrinkles, as though she threw them on as fast as possible in order to get to the computer.

From the outside, he looked emotionless, even machine-like. A rookie wouldn't be aware of the volcanic rage billowing beneath that calm exterior. Sakai took a step forward and saw the jumbled message on the computer screen.

"You know, Bordales, I can type a message of my own," he said. He slowly walked around her, speaking with a voice as cold as the void outside their hull. "It can say, 'To the Board of Department of Corrections and Rehabilitation, Private Morgan Bordales has failed to comply with the standards of the United World Order Marine Corps, and such, has failed to meet the expectations set for liberation. I hereby recommend she be discharged from active service and placed back into a holding facility and await further instructions from a judge.' What do you think, Private?"

Morgan didn't answer.

"I asked you a question," he snapped, voice raised, making her jolt slightly.

"Sir, that would be…unfavorable. Sir," she said. Her mind was in a whirlwind. She didn't know what else to say. Sakai completed his circle and stood nose to nose with her.

"I oughta write that message," he said. His voice was low now, which in a way was even worse. He glanced back at the computer screen and read the subject line. *To Jamie.* He'd seen it before. Even since Morgan came onto his unit, he had noticed an increased apprehension in her. She had lost custody of her son after she was convicted of drug smuggling. He heard the sob story that came with it; how hard it was to meet all of her expenses; how she couldn't afford education; yatta-yatta. It made him want to puke. He had seen the types of people she had worked with. Many of them were violent, dangerous people, whom he had led task force raids against. The law was right to take her kid away. The only reason she was allowed rehabilitation through military service was the fact that her defense attorney proved she played a non-violent role. According to the paperwork, she was only the shuttle driver. Still, he wasn't the biggest fan of the law change allowing certain felons the option to join active service. The idea of handing a firearm to someone of her background didn't sit right with him. Unfortunately, he didn't have much of a say in the matter.

Sakai cleared his throat. "Tell me why I shouldn't write that message."

"Because…" Morgan searched for words. "Because I'm trying to do better…sir!"

"What do you call better?" he asked. "You call dicking around in here when we're about to conduct a rescue operation *better*? Being late for drills, because you're too concerned with whether or not little Jamie got his birthday card? Is that better? Don't even get me started with your lack of attention and focus when on the job. Were you this incompetent as a white-root runner? Probably were, hence how easily you got caught."

"Yes, sir," she said. Better to say that than nothing at all.

"Bear in mind, Private, that the people we're trying to save from enemy hands don't give a shit about your personal issues. For all they care—for all I care, you've lost custody indefinitely. Hell, by the looks of it, he doesn't even want you around. And you might as well get over it, because the issue at hand is more important. Is that clear?"

The words stung and were nearly successful in inciting a reaction. Morgan wondered if it was because they were true.

"Is. That. Clear?" Sakai said.

"It is clear, Staff Sergeant," she answered.

"Good. Now get your goddamn gear and get your ass to briefing. You got two minutes, Private. That's one-two-zero seconds. Starting now! If you're not at that table at the end of it, I WILL write that message!"

Bordales hustled down the hall into briefing and took a left for the armory. She moved with the urgency instilled during boot camp. Luckily, her hurry spared her from noticing the disparaging stares from her teammates as she ran past them. Morgan entered the armory and grabbed a helmet. She tied her hair back as fast as she could. The permanent red dye would stand out like a sore thumb in the forest. It was another reminder of her outlaw days… and her stupidity. She would be stuck with the bright red hair for the rest of her life. Luckily, it was a color she liked. The military didn't have the same opinion, and considering the dye injection used, there would be no changing it. Being below standards, it almost kept her from enlisting. As Sakai once pointed out, she was screwing up in ways that even the Marine Corps couldn't fix.

Sixty seconds left.

Morgan tucked her hair into her helmet and strapped it shut, then slipped into her body armor. She grabbed a rifle off the rack, slapped in a mag, then holstered a standard Beretta sidearm.

Thirty-five seconds. She could hear Sakai's voice in her mind counting down the seconds. Knowing him, his threat was serious. She collected her knife and grenades. Morgan gave one last check over her supplies. She seemed to have everything but still felt she was missing something.

"Twenty seconds!" the Staff Sergeant's voice carried from down the hall. Now there was no doubt he was serious. Morgan hurried for the door and...

Spare magazine! She checked her armor pockets. None. Her role in the fight would be short without ammo, and Sakai's temper would be shorter. She spun on her heel and ran to the supply container, scooped up several mags, then ran for the hall, stuffing them in her pockets as she went.

"Six! Five! Four—" she felt as though he was deliberately counting fast. She sprinted and arrived in the briefing room at "One!" Morgan sucked in a deep breath through her nose and approached the table, trying to act as if nothing was wrong at all. The Staff Sergeant gave her one last glare, his blank stare a final warning to the marine. "Now that we're all present, let's get to the mission." He slipped a file chip into a slot in the table's console. A digital image of a stone-faced man hovered over the screen. He had a horseshoe-shaped scar over his left temple that traveled down to his ear. His head was shaved, his left eye pale. By the time this image was taken, his beard had had a few days of growth.

"This is Rutger Gillion, leader of the pirate gang *Red Nova*," Sakai explained.

"Did he have brain surgery or something?" Cutler asked, pointing at the scar.

"Why? You eager to operate?" Ward said.

"Marines," Sakai said, restoring order. "Minor skull fracture when hijacking a medical frigate in the Reg System. Unfortunately, he was able to get someone to patch him up. The good part of that is that it makes him easy to identify, and no plastic surgeon with credibility is gonna fix him up. Gillion might think he's tough shit, but he's no crime boss. He's just the head of a band of space pirates with limited supplies and weapons. He's a bluegill who thinks he's a great white. Taking them out will be a walk in the park for us. Target practice, really. The tricky part is getting in quietly and getting the hostages out alive. We're the only ship in the quadrant and backup won't arrive for another seventy-two to eighty-four hours. A lot can happen between now and then, so it's all on us."

"How many hostages, sir?" Vance asked. Ward snorted as he withheld a joke. *Shouldn't you say, comrade?*

"Four surveyors and geologists, with a crew of twenty led by Dr. Janet Saldivar and Dr. Martin Fry. Dr Fry was the one who sent the distress signal. According to his message, he was able to inject a microchip into his bloodstream. Now that we're in range, we're able to monitor his heart rate. Needless to say, he's alive. Basically, they came here at the wrong time, right as these bastards happened to be in the area. Their shuttle was hijacked but, as I stated before, Dr. Fry managed to get a distress signal out. That's why we're here. The pirates deactivated a tracker on the shuttle but not before we could pinpoint the location."

The image changed to a global landscape, which zoomed in to a patch of forest surrounding a mountain region. Sakai pointed to an area bordering a lake.

"The shuttle is here. Probably where they have the surveyors. One thing I know for certain is that there'll be a band of these pricks ransacking the shuttle. If the hostages are there, we'll nab them and get them to safety. If not, we'll kill whatever pirates we find except one, who we'll save for interrogation." He switched the image off and looked at his squad. "Any questions?"

"What does a simple band of pirates want with geologists?" Morgan asked. All eyes turned toward her.

"Well...for starters...they're pirates," Pinky said.

"Yeah," Ward added. "They steal shit. Kinda what pirates do."

"Yeah, but why keep them alive?" Morgan asked.

"Probably to navigate any informational data on the ship," Calloway said. His jaw moved as though munching on something. It was his urge to chew on some tobacco, but he would have to wait until they touched down on the planet.

"If you have any thoughts, Private, now's the time to spit them out," Sakai said. Morgan froze. She was already treading on thin ice with the Sergeant. She just couldn't help but think something was off about this pirate camp.

"It's just that it's odd they're settling *here* where there's no technology," she said. "Now they've got these surveyors hostage. There's been no ransom demands, has there?"

"No," Sakai answered. "Anything else?"

"I just feel like there's something going on that we don't know," Morgan said.

"Thank you, Private," Sakai said, "...for delaying us another thirty seconds, and for the non-info you've provided. From the info provided, the only items of value that was on their shuttle was fuel and supplies. No weapons, nothing that wound enhance the threat." Morgan swallowed. That thin ice was practically water right now.

There were no other questions from the team.

"Alright. Let's move," Sakai ordered.

****

14

The marines assembled at the dropship and harnessed themselves into their seats. Ward took the pilot's chair and activated the twin-ion-engines. The interior doors sealed, while the exterior doors opened.

Landon took the seat beside him. He always hated the shit-eating grin Ward wore when readying for takeoff.

"Please don't break the ship," he said. "Remember, we're trying to get down unseen."

"That's right," Sakai spoke through the commlink. *"Take us to point three-two-zero. That'll put us two miles from Circle Lake and allow us to approach unseen. They don't have atmosphere trackers, so they don't detect us coming in, unless you fly us down like a goddamn shooting star."*

"Oh, alright Sarge," Ward said.

In the cabin, Morgan tightened her harness and held her rifle close. She squeezed her eyes shut, her thoughts lost with good memories of Jamie. In her mind, he was still a three-year old toddler. With each recollection came the realization that he had grown so much since then. He was speaking full sentences now, attending school and making friends. She wondered what he was like now, and how well his father was doing with taking care of him. That brought another wave of guilt. It was a defensive instinct to think negative of her ex-husband, but the reality was he was the attentive, law-abiding parent who had his priorities in order. Only when Morgan had to pay the penalties for her actions did she gain some self-awareness. For a while, she blamed everyone but herself. And now she was here, a million lightyears away from the family she lost.

She opened her eyes and saw Sakai sitting across from her. She swallowed. How long had he been there?

"You still with us, Private?" he asked.

"Yes, sir," she said.

"You better be," he said. She read between the lines.

"I will be, sir," she said. She noticed he was looking at her outfit, specifically at her right hip.

"Got enough ammo?" he asked. Morgan's next breath was a shaky one.

"Gotta be prepared," she played it off.

"You could tuck one of those spare mags into your flashlight pocket, seeing as you didn't bother to grab one."

Shit! She flinched with the realization.

Ward's voice came through the comm. *"Alright, keep your fingers and toes in the vehicle at all times. We are a go!"* They could hear the groan of restraints lifting off the landing pads. Next was a slight shutter as the ship lifted off. The pilots engaged the thrusters. Morgan's back pressed deep into her seat as the ship soared out of the hangar bay and plunged down into Malek's atmosphere.

CHAPTER 3

Sweat and grime combined into a thin sludgy mixture that smeared across Dr. Janet Saldivar's otherwise golden skin. Her blond hair was peppered with dirt, as was her brown jumpsuit. The blowtorch added to the intense heat as she welded the patch over the shipping container.

"Go on, hurry it up," one of the pirates said. She felt the muzzle of his rifle goading her in the back. At first glance, those rifles sparked intense terror unlike anything she'd ever felt. But after two days of constant badgering and little sleep, she now felt the urge to spin around and fire the torch into his eyes. If she was the only hostage, she would probably resign herself to that fate.

Behind her was the pirate camp with twenty pirates wandering between their tents. Many of them wore jumpsuits stolen from the crew quarters of the *M. Cooper*. Others simply sported their typical sleeveless vests and worn cargo pants, which had all turned dark brown from overexposure to the elements without being washed. These pirates were no strangers to living minimally. Janet ventured a guess that they'd hit a string of bad luck, gaining little loot and payment, making them desperate. Also, judging by their depleted numbers, they probably suffered losses from conflicts, probably with other gangs.

To Janet's left was Chuck Cramer. Young and muscular, the twenty-four-year-old graduate student applied his torch to another armored plate. The metal was thick and needed a concentrated flame to get it to weld. It would take several minutes just to get a few millimeters together. Sweat was freefalling from his black hair. The camp was in a clearing, with no canopy to block out the sun's intense rays. He had stripped down to his tank top, his muscular arms now bright red from sunburn. Still, Chuck kept at the job, as it prevented the pirates from forcing Kim Harmon from doing the labor.

He allowed himself a moment to peek toward their ship, which had been set down about fifty meters to the north. Kim was in a loader, moving some of the pirates' supplies into the ship. The tracks kicked up dirt as she steered the two-ton vehicle out of the storage ramp. Because of the distance and the sun's glare on the windshield, he couldn't see her face, forcing him to visualize her short black hair, rectangular glasses, beach-tan skin, and of course, her smile. The smile he had to put extra effort into visualizing because there was nothing to smile about. There were at least four armed pirates watching her, and Chuck knew what thoughts were taking place in their sick minds.

"Hey! Eyes on your work," the pirate guard behind him said, pressing his rifle muzzle between Chuck's shoulder blades. Chuck resisted the urge to tell him off as he pressed the flame into the patch.

"How much longer?" someone spoke from within the camp. Janet recognized the pirate leader's husky voice.

"Might be a hundred years at the rate these fools work," one of the pirates answered. There was silence as Rutger Gillion stepped away from his tent and approached his captives. He stared and watched them conduct the repairs on the twelve-by-twelve containment box.

"You might have a point," he said. "Maybe I was wrong to keep these schoolboys alive. We could probably handle this payload ourselves."

"Good luck!" someone else called out in defiance.

Hearing Dr. Martin Fry's voice, Janet looked back, alert. *No, Martin, he'll beat you to a pulp…again.*

Martin Fry's face was covered in bruises. His left eye had been nearly swollen shut. He still wore the same plaid and blue jeans he had when they arrived. No matter how many centuries the human race endured, some fashions never changed. At fifty-three years old, he managed to land a few return blows to the gang that assaulted him, even managing to crack a few teeth. Then again, judging by the pirate gang's poor hygiene, dental or otherwise, that wasn't saying much.

The only pirate that was somewhat well-groomed was Gillion. His face was marked by several nicks from a recent shave. The skin around his big scar was blistered and his left eye white. He turned to look at Martin, tilting his face slightly to make him look into the lifeless white organ.

"Speak once more, Doctor, and I'll set my dogs on you a second time," he threatened. "Better yet, I'll set them on *her*." He pointed at Janet.

"Listen, Gillion," Martin said, "this isn't some backhoe or shuttle hull we're trying to fix. This is Europa-class steel made for containing highly radioactive material. The metal patches are made of the same stuff. It's very strong and takes a long time to patch with standard torches. If we had the right equipment, we'd have it done already."

"You have your friend to thank for that," Gillion snarled. Martin resisted the urge to pop him in the mouth. His friend and colleague, Dr. Henry Blake, knew what the pirates would do with their discovery. When the pirates infiltrated the ship and found the containment supplies, they learned that this expedition was not a simple survey job. During the initial survey of the planet, Dr. Blake and Fry were alerted to the discovery of a large uranium deposit. Even in this day and age, uranium and nuclear energy were valuable commodities. And now, it had fallen into Gillion's hands. Uranium sold for a high price on the black market, and Gillion was seeing dollar signs. With a box this size, he was seeing millions of them. The other two were already at the dig site, being loaded by Martin's dig crew. Both Martin and Janet were amazed that the bastards were even allowing the workers to wear the protective gear. For now, at least.

After the pirates brought the ship down to Malek's surface, Dr. Blake planted a demolition charge on the containment box. Before he could destroy the others, he was gunned down. His body was then thrown off a cliff somewhere to the east. Martin, his team, and his construction crew were kept alive, only to be used as slave labor.

Now, Martin and his survey team were undoing the damage Blake had done. It didn't take a Ph.D. to know that these pirates would kill the men once their use had worn out. And the women would fare even worse. The only thing that kept them untouched was the fact that they were being used as leverage to force everyone to work. Sadly, it was effective, despite knowing they were only delaying the inevitable. Luckily, Dr. Blake also managed to destroy the repair equipment before he was killed. With only standard welding torches, it would be a while before the repairs could be completed. All he could do was hope that his distress call was received and pray that rescue would come on swift wings.

"What? No witty comeback?" Gillion taunted the doctor. Martin didn't take the bait. He stepped away from the pirate and approached Janet. He could see a few black spots on her upper arms where some sparks had landed.

"Janet, take a break. I'll take over," he said.

"Martin, you need to rest," Janet said.

"I've rested plenty," he said.

"I'm fine," she protested.

"*Somebody* better get to work," Gillion shouted. "One way or another, this chitchat's gonna end." Martin turned to face him.

"They need a break," he said. "You've been working them for hours."

"Sooner they finish, the sooner they'll be done," Gillion replied. Martin knew what that meant. His eyes went to the sky.

Please God, send someone to help us.

"It's almost done," Chuck said, in hopes of calming the situation.

"How long?" Gillion said.

"I don't know. Maybe..." Chuck stammered as Gillion stomped his way over to him, clearly unhappy with the answer. "One hour!" Gillion looked up at the patches. There was seven inches of metal that still needed to be patched.

"Boy, it took you two hours to do half of that?!"

"Okay, maybe a little longer," Chuck said.

"We'll have it done! And you'll have your precious uranium," Janet snapped. Gillion looked at her and grinned.

"You're feisty for a geologist," he said. "I like that." He stared at her, eyeing her muscular figure, then finally stepped away, bumping Martin in the process. "If this isn't done by sundown, I'll reunite all of you with Doctor-what's-his-name. I'm sure the bugs living in that gorge will be delighted to have your company." Martin waited for him to move behind a firing line of three pirates, then approached Janet.

"Janet, don't push these guys too far," he whispered.

"Martin, it's been two days," she said. "Nobody's come." Martin put a finger in her face to make it appear to the guards he was scolding her.

"Christ, Janet, it's a new planet. There's no base around here. It'll take a couple days for anyone to get all the way out here, even in hyperspace." He glanced back to make sure he wasn't heard. "Someone will come. I promise. Just delay these repairs as long as you can. As long as they need us, they won't—you know." Janet shook her head. "What? Don't you trust me?"

"Of course, I trust you, Martin," she said. "I'm sorry. It hasn't been an easy couple of days."

"Hey, you think it hasn't been rough on all of us?" Martin asked. She looked at his bruised face and forced a smile.

"It's an improvement," she said. The two of them shared a moment of levity, which came to an abrupt end when the guards started shouting at them.

"Quit the chatter!"

"Alright, alright," Martin said. A thunderous boom echoed from the shuttle, drawing everyone's attention. Smoke was trailing from the loader's engine. Kim Harmon, in a panic, put the vehicle in reverse in an attempt to lock the brake in place. The vehicle sped backward, slamming a second time into the shuttle's bulkhead.

Pirates swarmed around her like ants to a worm.

"Shit!" Martin said. "She jammed the gears. Chuck, go help her! You're better with machinery than I am."

"But what about…"

"I'll take over welding. You just go check on Kim. Hurry." Chuck handed Martin the torch and goggles and hopped off the ladder. The pirates pointed their rifles at him.

He raised his hands. "I'm just going over to help Kim! She's not familiar with the loader like I am." *She's not familiar with any kind of mechanical equipment.* The pirates cautiously lowered their weapons.

"Fine. Hurry up," one of them said. Chuck ran across the field to the loader. The guards yanked the platform door open, shouting at her.

"Hey, holdup!" he said, keeping his hands raised and voice calm. "Let me look! I might be able to fix it." One of the pirates glared at him.

"You better, tool."

"He can't be much worse than this useless bitch," one of the others growled. They climbed off the loader and made way for him. Chuck waved his hand to blow away some of the smoke. The air stank of charred oil. These loaders took Grade-C diesel fuel, as opposed to Grade-D which the speeders used. One of the workers must've installed the wrong kind. He climbed onto the tracks and opened the door.

Kim Harmon was frozen in fear. Her eyes were misty and her teeth were clenched.

"It's alright. It's not your fault," he said. He gently pried her hands from the levers. Her muscles were almost as rigid as a corpse. The bastard pirates probably threatened her in ways he didn't want to imagine. He noticed she was looking down. That's when he realized she wasn't wearing her glasses. They must've fallen off during the accident. He knelt down and found them near the brake pedal. "Here you go," he said, placing them on her face. Kim finally started to loosen up.

"I don't know what happened. I was driving the thing and all of a sudden—"

"I think I know what happened," he interrupted. "Mind stepping out and letting me take over?" She was halfway out before he finished speaking. She hated machines. Of all people to operate this thing, the pirates chose her. Chuck took the driver's seat and tried re-starting the engine. It groaned and rumbled. He heard the clattering of loose parts while more smoke poured from the crack. Chuck shut it down and stepped out, just in time to see Gillion marching over.

"What did you fools do?" he shouted.

"The loader's dead," Chuck said.

"Don't bullshit me. You spent less than ten seconds inspecting it."

"Look here!" Chuck pointed to the engine. "It's cracked. And I think you know smoke coming from this part of any vehicle is a bad thing."

"So, the bitch broke it," Gillion said. He drew his pistol and pointed it at Kim. Chuck quickly stepped in front of her.

"The wrong oil was installed in it," he shouted.

"So what?"

"Well, the wrong oil can lead to reduced lubrication and shorter engine life. Automotive One-oh-one. That's exactly what happened here. No surprise too, considering the heat. The oil broke down, causing too much metal-on-metal friction. The gears couldn't rotate properly. The serpentine belt's probably messed up. The engine block's probably cracked."

"Then fix it," Gillion said.

"I—I can't," Chuck said. "The parts aren't here. You took them to the dig site with the other loader." Gillion waited for a moment, keeping his pistol fixed on the graduate student. After several tense moments, he lowered it, then spoke into his commlink.

"Base camp to Bannister, come in," he said. He waited for a response. Nothing. "Base camp to Bannister. Come in, goddamnit." There was still no response. "Fucking pricks don't answer their commlink!" He turned and shouted at the tents. "Rico!" He waited a moment. "Rico! Get your ass over here!" A towering figure emerged from the back of the camp and hustled into the plains like a dog.

"Yes, Gillion?" Rico said. The pirate was the biggest in the entire group. He had a crooked nose and a square jaw that was slightly crooked.

"Have you heard anything from the dig site?"

"Negative. They never completed their ten-hundred check-in, either."

"Communications are always bad around there," one of the other pirates said.

"I don't recall asking you," Gillion snapped. The pirate swiftly turned away. Seething, Gillion leaned toward Rico. "Could it be a comm failure?"

"It's possible," Rico said. "I tried having someone in Camp B make a call, but they can't get ahold of them either." Gillion groaned.

"We need their loader," he said. "There's no other choice. Go out there on a speeder and bring their loader back. We won't be able to load up that containment box without it."

"I'm on my way now," Rico said. The pirate hurried to the tree line and shouted at his fellow pirates. "You four, come with me!" They grabbed rifles and boarded one of the Humvees. The driver started the engine then looked to Rico for directions.

"Which route?"

"Take us northwest. We'll stop by Camp B for a moment and check if they've made any contact," Rico said. The driver nodded and steered the vehicle into the forest. In seconds, they disappeared behind the wall of trees.

Janet listened to the disruption of wildlife as the Humvee sped off. She leaned over toward Martin Fry.

"Something's off," she said. "They've had no communication problems since we arrived." Martin nodded slightly.

"No, they haven't," he said. They shared a glance, mirroring each other's optimism. Perhaps there was a different reason the dig site wasn't responding. Whatever it was, Janet was feeling a little more confident about that distress call Martin had sent out.

Seeing the impatient expressions on the guards, they got back to work.

Janet pressed the flame to the steel, gradually melting the edges of the patch. Her stomach began to tighten, her optimism replaced by a sense of dread and guilt. The military better respond, or else all they were doing was helping the pirates get the uranium off the planet. And who knew who'd they sell it to. Knowing how far these pirates were on the 'scum-level', it would be nobody good.

She glanced at the sky, hopeful to see signs of a ship's descent. Instead, she saw nothing but clear blue sky.

Come on, where's the damn calvary? her anxious mind wondered.

"Taking a break?" the guard asked. Janet flipped him the bird then returned to work.

CHAPTER 4

It had been twenty minutes since touchdown. The marines were now deep in the forest heading northeast toward Dr. Fry's signal. They moved two-by-two, each duo keeping a dozen feet apart from the next. Sakai was in front. To his left was Pinky. His sniper rifle was slung over his back in favor of his submachine-gun.

"I could settle in a place like this," he muttered. "Build a cabin by the lake. Get an old-fashioned cane pole. Hook up some fish…"

"I didn't ask," Sakai said. They continued patrolling for a few more minutes, hearing the distant bird calls. It was almost identical to the forests in Maine, with a few unfamiliar species of trees added to the maples and pines. There were trees with elongated leaves that resembled the arms of an octopus. Most of the species were bright green except for a type that resembled maple leaves, which had a brownish-red pigmentation.

"Just saying…" Pinky continued. "I'm kind-of an outdoors guy at heart. I can see myself being among the first settlers here."

"Keep talking and you'll get your wish," Sakai said.

"You'd miss me," Pinky said.

"As much as I'd miss liver cancer," Sakai said.

"Aww, Sarge, I have feelings you know," Pinky said. Sakai held up a fist, signaling for the group to stop. They spread out and crouched low, weapons at the ready. Sakai studied the ground with his fingers. He peeled down flattened grass from the dirt, revealing a print. Pinky's expression turned serious. "Pirate patrol?"

"These ones yes," Sakai said. He pointed out several more prints in the dirt. "I'd estimate a group of four."

"You sound concerned," Pinky pointed out.

"About the patrol? No. It's this that's bothering me." Sakai moved up ahead to the next tree over. There were bullet holes in the trunk.

"Looks like they had something of a skirmish," Pinky said.

"Yeah. But with what?" Sakai said. The bullet holes were twelve-feet high, centered near a large branch connected with the trunk. Using hand signals, Sakai ordered the marines to spread out. Morgan, Ward, and Hood moved to the right. Cutler and Landon moved further ahead then turned left, while Vance and Calloway watched the team's six.

Sakai backed up for a better view. He could see grooves in the branch caused by edged objects. They were in rows of three, each mark separated by a few inches. Near these grooves were bullet holes scattered in the tree. Whatever had caused these marks, the pirates were compelled to shoot at it. That wasn't saying much: they were pirates, after all. They'd trap minnows in a bucket and shoot them just for the cheap sense of superiority.

"We have casings over here," Landon said. Sakai saw them about forty yards to his ten-o'clock.

"Ward, take Morgan and Hood and follow the trail. See where it leads. Use commlinks to update us," he said. He hustled over to join up with Landon and Cutler, along with Vance and Calloway.

Cutler was standing near a tree. Sakai immediately saw the bullet holes. Like the other tree, they were high up. Something had been perched high on a branch, and whatever it was, the pirates felt compelled to shoot it. He would've brushed it off as them shooting some birds or tree-dwelling mammals until he saw the large grooves embedded in the trunk. Something large had climbed up the tree.

"Any bodies?" he asked.

Landon shook his head. "No bodies, sir. Just this." He picked up the pirate rifle and offered it to the Staff Sergeant. It was a Sinkev Model-40, containing an elongated barrel for straight accurate shooting. It was lightweight with a forty-round mag inserted in the bottom. Sakai inspected the weapon. There were three scrapes on the left side of the barrel, as though someone had swung a pitchfork at it. He removed the magazine and ejected the remaining rounds. Ten.

"Those casings probably came from this gun," he said.

"Maybe something on this planet is doing our job for us," Landon said.

"Perhaps," Sakai said.

"Is that blood?" Vance said, pointing at a brown smear in the grass near the casings. Sakai knelt down to inspect. It was definitely blood, roughly a few hours old. Whether it was human or animal, he had no way to know for sure. What he did know, was that a struggle had taken place. The grass was flattened, the dirt kicked up all around the casings.

Whatever attacked them was large enough to overpower a grown man and wrestle him to the ground.

"God, who knows what kind of wildlife is on this planet," Cutler said. He started sanitizing his hands.

"Oh, for chrissake, Doc," Sakai groaned.

"I'm telling you, sir," Cutler said, "there's all kinds of shit here that we don't know about. I don't even want to get into the poisonous species of plants that might be here. Or what diseases the wildlife carries. We should've brought our protective suits." He proceeded to rub disinfectant on his neck and face.

"You know Doc, I don't have any advanced degree—" Calloway said.

"You don't say," Cutler interrupted.

"*But*...I'm pretty sure this pirate wasn't killed by some illness. I think you'll be fine," Calloway finished.

"Of course, *you'd* be fine. You're immune to everything. You were literally born in a barn," Cutler said. "Of course, you might not be immune to whatever the mosquitos are carrying. There could be infections that'll melt your skin off. Hell, there might even be species on this planet that'll lay eggs in your veins, which'll root in your organs and grow into huge maggot creatures."

"And hand sanitizer will certainly save you from that," Calloway quipped.

"Settle down, Marines," Sakai said.

"Serious question," Vance said. "Why would they leave a perfectly functional rifle behind?"

"And what the hell were they shooting at?" Landon added.

"It's a relatively new planet. There could be some dangerous wildlife here," Sakai said. He looked at the gun again, then at the casings. Vance had a good point: pirates weren't the type to leave weapons lying around. It made him wonder, what became of the rest of the patrol?

He inspected the tracks again. There were several boot prints. He had predicted four a few minutes ago. The discovery of the rifle and blood now suggested there were originally five. The tracks, like the blood, were hours old. The group seemed to be walking in a standard formation, just a few feet apart from each other. Then, all of a sudden, they spun around. There were a few shell casings scattered about, nothing compared to the large grouping near the bloodstain. It seemed these other pirates turned, saw their companion go down, fired a few shots, then ran. From what?

That's when he noticed the other prints in the dirt. They were clawed in appearance, definitely not human. The toes were long and narrow like a lizard's. Though oddly enough, whatever it was, didn't appear to walk on four legs. Each print was in sets of two. It made him think of the feet of an ostrich. At least, it appeared to move like one.

"These tracks are everywhere," Cutler said. Sakai saw him pointing at a group coming from the north. He saw Vance and Calloway pointing out some faint tracks coming from the west.

Now it made sense why the pirates ran. They had encountered a pack of animals. Carnivorous animals that had no fear of the sound of gunfire. And judging by the fact that there were no bodies, Sakai suspected these things were fast, agile, and very stealthy.

****

Ward's group followed the trail for a few hundred yards. All three marines cautiously watched their surroundings. Morgan was growing tense. They had discovered signs that the enemy was nearby. She had been in a dozen firefights and had never gotten used to them.

"Hey, *Little Mermaid*. Your hair's poking out of your helmet," Hood whispered to her.

"Damn," she muttered. She slung her rifle over her shoulder and fixed it. Otherwise, it might as well serve as a bullseye out here.

"You want fancy hair, you should get a mohawk like mine," Ward joked.

"No thanks," Morgan replied. She tucked her hair firmly beneath her helmet then ran her fingers along the edges for any loose strands. They continued to follow the tracks. They had spread further apart, with greater distance between each stride. The pirates were running, not patrolling. After several more meters, the tracks moved in completely separate directions. Whatever happened here, it was every man for himself.

"We got a rifle here," Hood said. Morgan and Ward caught up to him and observed the weapon. It lay in the middle of battered ground concluding the trail of one set of tracks. The grass around it was uprooted and flattened. There were strands of blood-soaked clothing tossed about.

"I'm no tracker, but I don't think whoever this was simply took a bullet and fell," Ward said. "There was a tussle of some kind. Whatever was sitting in those trees chased this guy and pinned him down."

"Whatever it was, it was able to freak them out enough to make them scatter," Morgan said.

"You look like *you're* about to freak out," Ward said to her, grinning. The acknowledgement worsened her anxiety. Morgan could feel sweat soaking her fatigues. The intense heat was not making it better.

"Let's keep going," Hood said. "Morgan, you take the right. See where those tracks lead." They pressed on. Morgan made sure to keep within visual distance as she followed the set of tracks that veered to the right. They were hard to follow, especially with the terrain and the distance between strides.

She noticed some markings in the ground, trailing a few feet beside the human footprints. It was like someone had marked the ground with a series of razors. Whatever caused them was much heavier than a human. She continued for another few yards until she arrived at the edge of the hill. She looked down the slope and saw that the tracks ended near some thick bushes roughly twenty feet down.

She glanced over her shoulder to make sure she could see her fellow marines. She could only catch glimpses of them behind the trees. They had moved a couple hundred feet further to the east. Now, they were inspecting something in the grass. Probably another rifle. The thought of which made Morgan wonder if there was a weapon remaining at the end of this trail. She shouldered her weapon and proceeded down the hill.

A ghastly smell filled her nostrils. There were mosquitos and flies buzzing over the bushes. Morgan slowed. Something didn't feel right. She regretted proceeding any further without backup. Her gut tightened. It was a feeling she experienced during her drug shipping days, particularly the day she was caught. It was a sensation that she was being watched.

She noticed several dark smears on the side of the bush. At first, she thought it might had been the natural pigmentation of the plant. Then she saw the thick, coagulated puddle soaking the soil below, and the empty pistol in the middle of it. The slide was locked back, with several empty cartridges all around.

She slowly approached. Now, her eye was looking down the rifle's iron sights. Her finger rested on the trigger, ready to squeeze at any movement. She approached the brush.

There was a mass on the ground behind it. The swarm of flies had grown so thick it was practically a cloud hovering over the brush. Morgan moved in a semicircle along the left side. Behind the bushes were strips of clothing. There was a boot laying on its side. There was something sticking out of it…a bone. Morgan leaned in and pushed the branches aside.

A swarm of flies erupted from the ground, uncovering the skeletal remains. They were human, definitely a member of the pirate gang. There were remnants of tactical gear tossed away along with some more clothing. Morgan backed away. Her stomach rolled at the sight of the bare skull staring back at her. There were strands of flesh remaining where the cheeks had been. The eye sockets were empty, though the skin along the forehead remained. The pirate's long hair was sprawled out behind the skull, stretching along the ground. Several of the ribs had been broken off. Fingers were missing from the one remaining hand. The other was nowhere to be seen. Pieces of meat had littered the ground. The body was mostly empty. There were no organs other than a few pieces of intestine. Everything had been stripped away, and done so violently.

Her anxiety intensified, as did the tightening of her stomach. Although now it was probably due to nausea. At that moment, a heavy breeze swept through the forest, rustling all the branches above her. Her heart fluttered. It felt as though the damn forest was toying with her. The swaying branches created moving shadows along the forest floor. It was like an army of black figures dancing around her. Each moving piece gave Morgan suspicion. She crouched slightly and watched her surroundings, ready to sprint at the first sign of danger.

The breeze died down. The rustling continued for a few seconds after, then dissipated into silence. Suddenly, she was aware of the putrid smell again. The flies buzzed back down, eager to feed upon the scraps. Morgan covered her mouth and backed away. The other marines would need to know about this.

"Sergeant," she said. There was no response. She realized she hadn't activated the commlink in her helmet. "Shit!" She felt along her helmet for the button to activate it.

Something snapped behind her. She heard a small branch hit the ground. Something was in the tree. She heard the creaking of branches and rustling of leaves, gradually descending downward. Morgan's mind immediately recalled the gunshot markings Sakai had discovered on the trees. Whatever killed these pirates was hiding in the trees.

And now it had found her.

Everything that followed was a blur. Morgan spun on her heel and aimed high. She saw the shape moving behind a wall of leaves. She fired. Thunderous cracks echoed through the forest. Flocks of birds took to the sky. Leaves and bark rained down as a large mass fell from the branches, right onto Morgan. She let out a scream as it drove her to the ground.

****

Sakai spun to his right and aimed his rifle. His marines took firing positions near trees, ready to engage the threat. The gunshots were definitely from a VR Rifle. The Sinkevs had a slower rate of fire and duller sounding discharges as opposed to the machine-like sound of the VRs. As fast as it came, the shooting stopped.

"Report contact," Sakai said. The comm was silent for several moments.

"False alarm, Sarge." It was Ward's voice. *"We have ourselves a champion monkey shooter. Trophy goes to the redhead."*

Sakai shook his head, muttering, "Fuck, you've got to be kidding me." He then spoke up, "Alright, we're on our way." He waved a finger and pointed forward, gesturing for all his marines to push on. "This way. And no wasting ghosts."

They continued onward. Each marine was now on alert. Hopefully, the shooting hadn't alerted the pirates of their presence, or worse, put the hostages in any danger.

They followed the trail and found Pvt. Hood waiting for them. His grenade launcher was slung over his shoulder. He pointed to his left with the muzzle of his submachine gun.

"Over there," he said.

"Keep watch. Pharris, wait here with him. You have eyes like a hawk," Sakai said.

"And the teeth of a chipmunk," Hood added.

"Fuck your mother," Pinky retorted. The two of them kept watch while the squad moved in on the hill. They found Ward helping Morgan to her feet. On the ground beside them was a four-foot long primate. Its chest and stomach had been torn open by the explosive-tip rounds from Morgan's rifle.

"Well done, convict," he said. "Why don't you just fly a banner across the sky that says, *Hey Gillion! We're here now!*"

"I saw movement in the trees," Morgan said, stammering over her words. "I thought it was the thing that killed the pirates."

"Probably had it coming," Ward said. "Up in the canopy, watching you…he probably was having some very dirty thoughts." He looked over at Cutler, who was looking bothered as he always did. "What? Don't tell me you're about to go all germaphobe on me again."

The doctor pointed at the bushes.

"What the hell is that?"

The marines gathered around the remains. Some exclaimed disgust, while Calloway spit a glob of chewing tobacco. It landed right in one of the eye sockets.

"Score," he said. There were a few chuckles from the group, though most were shaky. Though they wouldn't admit it, they no longer felt a harsh criticism of Morgan's actions. After piecing together the incident, they all probably would've reacted similarly.

"Holy shit. What the hell did this?" Landon said.

"Whatever it was, it stripped this bastard right down to the bone," Vance said. She spoke something in Russian, shaking her head at the corpse. "Forest demon."

"Don't get religious on us now," Ward said.

"This is why we have surveys before colonizing planets," Sakai said. "Marines, be on the lookout. There's something in these woods. It's tasted human flesh now. And judging by these remains, and everything lacking, I'd say it likes the taste."

"I'll say," Calloway said. He knelt down by the bones and reached by the shoulder joint. Cutler swatted flies, watching in disgust as the stocky marine grabbed something and pulled.

"What the hell are you doing?" he asked. Calloway tugged harder and pried the thing loose. He held it up to Sakai. It was a curved tooth, light-brown in color with a serrated edge.

"Holy shit, that's nearly two inches long," Cutler said.

"Did the initial inspection of the planet discover any species like this?" Morgan asked. "I only recall reading that the only carnivorous species in this region were feline." Sakai cocked his head.

"No," Sakai said. "Like you said, only feline species. But initial inspections always miss things. It's hard to do a planet-wide survey, even with satellite scanners. Too many species to document at once. The main purpose of the surveys is to determine what levels of terraforming are needed and whether there's any toxins or bacteria in the air."

"Don't know about you, but it's not the bacteria I'm worried about," Cutler said.

"That's a first," Vance said.

"Look sharp, Marines," Sakai said. "We've got more than pirates to watch out for. Vance, Ward, watch our six. Don't draw too close to the trees. Watch for any movement. Calloway, take point."

The marines moved up the hill, the farm boy moving several meters ahead. After rejoining with Hood and Pinky, they proceeded northeast.

CHAPTER 5

Rico bounced in his seat as the Humvee tore through the forest. The driver knew Gillion was growing impatient, which spelled bad news if they took too long to get word to the dig site. Under less pressing circumstances, Rico would have him take the vehicle straight north then turn west at the rock plains, but that would've added another forty-five minutes to their trip.

Griswold, the Humvee's driver, veered sharply to the right, barely avoiding collision with the trees.

"Stupid moron," Rico sneered.

"You told me to hurry up," Griswold said. Rico sucked in a breath.

"Okay, yes I did," he admitted. "Just, slow it down a bit."

"Gonna have to anyway," Griswold said. "We're getting close to Camp B."

"Good," Rico said. "This is higher elevation. I'm gonna try again to radio the dig site." He pulled out a hand-held commlink and raised it to his lips. "Rico to Bannister. Come in." He waited for a response. There was nothing.

"It's these trees, man," one of the three passengers said. Griswold wasn't sure whether it was Gatton, Bolden, or Dymonte. The damn engine was too loud, a sign of the crude technology the pirates were forced to scavenge.

"It's not these trees," Rico growled. "Yeah, they screw with the signal, but not to this extent. Usually after the second or third try, we're able to get a response. Either it's a technical issue, or Bannister's fucking around. If he is, he's gonna find himself buried in that uranium pit."

"What about Camp D? Anyone try them?" Griswold asked. Rico swallowed. Luckily Gillion wasn't here to witness this conversation. He'd chastise Rico as a fool for not thinking of contacting the camp guarding the shuttles. The ships' receivers were by far the best in the whole gang.

"Rico to Camp D, come in," he said. There was no response. "The fuck? Camp D, answer your goddamn comm." He threw the comm on the dashboard. "What the hell's going on?! Where the hell is everybody?"

"Jerking around, probably," Griswold said.

"No, I mean...where is everybody?" Rico said. "We should've come across some of our patrols by now. Where are the perimeter guards?" They watched the forest in silence. "Are you sure we're close?"

"I've driven this route a few dozen times, boss," the driver said. "There's the crooked tree we marked for reference when we first set up the camp. We should be there in just a couple of minutes."

The pirates rode in silence for the remainder of the trip. Rico watched the trees passing by the window, searching for any perimeter guards. Instead, it was as though the forest was void of life.

Something hit the windshield, causing Griswold to nearly jump from his seat.

"SHIT!"

Rico faced forward, rifle pointed, ready to blast holes at whatever was assaulting the vehicle. A greenish mixture spread across the glass, trailing black shards of exoskeleton.

"Damn bug!" the driver said, watching one of the severed wings sliding down the green river. Goliath beetles were harmless, but quite the nuisance, especially when driving. Their seven-inch bodies had enough fluid in them to fill a water jug. And right now, all those contents were spread across the windshield, forcing the driver to slow to a stop or else risk smashing into a tree. He activated the wipers, which only served to smear the guts across the glass. The hundred-degree heat caked the blood to the windshield. "Son of a bitch." All these advancements in technology, and the human race still couldn't graduate from the primitive design of windshield wipers.

The driver sat dumbfounded, uncertain of what to do.

"What are you waiting for?" Rico said. "Get out there and scrape it off, you idiot." The other pirates chuckled as their companion stumbled out of his seat and grabbed a jug of cleaner from the back. He poured it over the left side of the windshield then scrubbed with a cloth. Slowly, the caked blood started to come apart like melting ice. The pirate climbed over the hood to reach the center.

Rico crossed his arms and waited. He watched the green mixture thin and come apart. After several seconds, the glass began to clear. Rico watched as a section was wiped away, wide enough so he could see his subordinate on the other side.

"You'd make a nice cleaning lady," Dymonte shouted. The group broke into laughter. Even Rico allowed a smile to show through. It immediately disappeared. As more of the glass cleared, he could see something behind the driver.

The pirate noticed his leader's shocked expression, and those of the other pirates. It was right then when he heard the sounds of breathing and movement. Something was behind him. He grabbed his pistol and spun around, but only got halfway before the attacker was on him. Spring-like legs catapulted the creature, throwing all three hundred pounds of its weight onto him.

The pirates shouted in terror and confusion as it pinned their companion to the hood. It was reptilian in appearance, standing on two back legs which were not denting the vehicle's hood downward. Three-fingered hands slashed Griswold's faces, ripping him from both temples all the way down to his chin. Blood splattered over the glass. The pirate raised his hands to defend himself, only to scream as the jaws clamped down over his right forearm. What followed was a blur of motion as the beast shook its head side-to-side, all while raking its claws over Griswold's body. Bones popped and flesh tore, releasing a crimson fountain over the windshield.

Rico and his pirates poured out of the vehicle. Bolden and Dymonte took the left side, Rico and Gatton on the right. In the brief moment it took to disembark, the creature had yanked its head backward. With a sickening sound, Griswold's arm detached.

Fleshy strands dangled from the creature's mouth as it panned its angular head. It saw humans on both sides of the transport baring their strange loud weapons. It dropped the arm and sprang to the right, throwing itself into the two pirates grouped near the driver's side. Its feet struck dead center on one's chest, driving him to the ground. It slashed its tail, striking Dymonte across the face and sending him spiraling several times before falling.

Bolden let out a scream, which escalated into an agonized howl as two eight-inch claws burrowed their way into his chest. The beast drove its fingers into his shoulders, holding him in place as it raked both feet down his body. Blood spurted from his mouth and stomach as the sickle-shaped claws ripped him open from the chest to his pelvis.

Dymonte staggered to his feet, his face red from where he had been struck. He spun to face the threat and shouldered his rifle. His friend had already been torn wide open. Blood, entrails, and various chunks of meat were scattered everywhere. Rico hurried around the hood of the Humvee, his muzzle pointed at the lizard.

He fired twice. The creature shrieked and ran through the forest with the speed of a jackrabbit.

"Fuck!" Rico shouted. He wasn't sure if he hit the thing or not. Whatever it was, it was fast. And strong. For something to have such speed, the muscles in its legs had to contain the strength of a mustang.

"What the hell was that?" Gatton shouted.

"I know what it was: a fucking dinosaur!" Dymonte replied. Had Rico not seen the thing, he'd recommend Dymonte be put before a firing squad for suggesting such lunacy. But he did see it. He had seen sketches of it before his life of crime. On Earth, there were museums displaying reconstructed skeletons of prehistoric beasts. He had seen one with the same shape and pose as the monster had when it killed Griswold. There was a chart containing information about the specimen, most of it he couldn't remember. The only word that stuck out to him was the subgroup: Raptor.

Movement in the trees caught his attention. Rico looked up and saw a cloud of leaves bursting from the branch as a large mass descended. Its arms were reared back, its feet tucked under its body, claws protruding. Dymonte heard its deep roar, then felt its feet come down on his shoulders. Next thing he knew, he was face down in the dirt. Pain surged through his body as the claws slit his flesh in a bike-pedaling motion.

More roars echoed from the forest. Rico could hear the sounds of running feet closing in. There were more. They were all around him. Rico couldn't see them, but felt their presence. He didn't even give a thought of helping Dymonte. At this point, it was every man for himself. He turned and ran ahead of the Humvee. A few feet behind him was Gatton, who carried the same mindset. They tore through bushes and tall grass in a desperate attempt to make it to the pirate camp.

"Almost there?" Gatton called out.

"Yes. Just run!" Rico shouted back.

"But how far?!"

"Shut up and run!"

"What if those things have—AGH!!!"

Rico gave a quick glance over his shoulder. All he saw were two tails pointed skyward, thrashing back and forth as two raptors wrestled Gatton to the ground. His screams were muffled by the sounds of flesh ripping and bones snapping.

Rico kept running. Sweat spilled from his face like rain. The anxiety had caused an ache in his chest and stomach. There was forest all around him, blinding his field of view. He swung his rifle back and forth, nervously expecting a raptor to come jumping out at him at any moment.

Finally, he saw tents. Camp B was less than a hundred feet ahead. Rico doubled his pace, closing the distance and leaping the final ten feet. He landed in a clearing on the edge of the campsite. There were two tents directly in front of him obscuring his vision. All he could see up ahead was a fireplace and kettle surrounded by makeshift seats made of rocks and logs. There were no pirates there to greet him. No movement or sound of any kind.

"Hey! Anyone here?!" he called out. There was no answer. He passed between the two large tents and stepped into the center of the camp. He shuddered, his trembling hands struggling to hold onto the rifle. Camp B was in ruins. Blood was everywhere. There were two bodies to the left that had been stripped down to the bone. Flies and mosquitos buzzed throughout the camp, hoping to get a bite out of the carcasses left behind in the raptors' wake.

Shell casings littered the ground. Rifles and supplies were scattered everywhere. The tents to his left were collapsed, the tarps slashed open. The kettle was full, the logs beneath it burnt to ash. The attack had likely taken place the previous night.

Now it made sense why all comms went down. These attacks were happening everywhere. There was nobody left to check-in with.

Rico heard movement behind him. He turned and knelt into a firing position, then waited. The sounds stopped. He glanced up into the trees. There was nothing there he could see. Then again, the branches were so thick, he probably wouldn't know if there were a hundred of those things gathered up there. He waited for several more seconds. There was no movement, nor any sounds to be heard other than the buzzing of flies.

Reality started to dawn on him. He could not wait here forever. All he was doing was prolonging the inevitable. There was no defense against these horrific creatures. They were too fast, cunning, and had an advantage in numbers. His best chance at survival was to flee.

Rico thought fast. While carefully keeping watch of his surroundings, he thought of the layout of the camp. He remembered Camp B parked their vehicles behind the tree line on the east side, which was behind him. He slowly backed across the camp, keeping mild pressure on the rifle trigger. As he closed in on the east perimeter, he turned around. He stepped over the tents. His heart pounded harder as he approached the tree line. He could only see a few yards past it, and the only thing visible was forest. In a way, that was worse than looking those lizards straight in the face.

He stopped at the trees, hesitated for a moment, then stepped out of the camp. So far, nothing. He stepped further out. He could see the log fence they made to mark the vehicle space. There was only one motorcycle standing upright. Two others had fallen, their dashboards smothered in blood. Several yards back was the camp's Jeep. It had smashed into a tree, the engine completely destroyed. The windshield was shattered and the driver's side window splattered from the inside with red.

Rico hopped on the only standing bike and started its engine. To his relief, it started. There was movement behind him. He glanced back and saw the reptilian shapes entering the camp. His eyes went up. A single branch on one of the trees was shaking. Rico couldn't see anything, but it was obvious the wind wasn't doing that.

He gunned the motorcycle, kicking up dirt as he sped into the forest. As soon as he went, the raptor made its jump, landing in the space he had just been. Rico let out a laugh. He glanced back. It didn't appear to be chasing him. He laughed again, rejoicing in how he outsmarted the lizards.

"You'll have to work for this meal!" he shouted. He weaved past several trees, then laughed again. A high-pitched shriek drowned out his merriment and turned it into a scream. By the time he saw the raptor directly in front of him, it had already jumped. The motorcycle rode off without him as he was tackled out of his seat. Rico screamed and tried to push it away. Razor teeth closed on his hand, severing all fingers except his thumb. It raked one of its feet across his belly horizontally, then ripped away a large strip of inedible clothing, exposing the gaping incision. Rico gurgled his last breaths, feeling his intestines being violently ripped from his abdomen. Before his vision faded to permanent black, the raptor gazed down at him, with a bloody rib bone sticking out of its teeth.

It dropped the bone, licked its chops, then lunged downward with gaping jaws.

CHAPTER 6

Muscles strained as the jaw minced the meat. Chuck Cramer winced. The food breaks the pirates gave him were almost worse than being forced to work. It was the leftovers from some local species of bird they hunted. It was a few days old, and he suspected it wasn't cooked very well to begin with. Also, the pricks forgot to pull out the little bones.

Chuck spit into the fire, then wiggled his tongue to make sure he got the little shard out. Kim Harmon was sitting to his right. There was a plate of beans and bird meat, hardly touched.

"I know you're more of a vegetarian, but it's important you keep your strength up," he whispered.

"Why?" she said. "Why waste the food? They're gonna kill us anyway." Cramer took a breath. *Yeah, they probably will.*

He heard one of the pirates shouting obscenities at Janet Saldivar, who was seated with Martin across the fireplace. She had finished her meager rations and was trying to absorb the few minutes of peace before being forced to work again. Of course, the pirate to notice was Craggy, which triggered his superiority complex. He prodded her with his rifle.

"Fine, I'm getting up, you acne-faced llama," she said. Craggy sneered and continued prodding her as she stood up. Martin sprang to his feet and put himself between them.

"Give it a rest, why don't ya?!" he said. Craggy rammed the rifle into his midsection, dropping him to his knees.

"Keep it up, and I'll prod her with something else. And I'll make you watch!" Craggy said. The thought made all four surveyors turn green with disgust. Janet stood, her eyes flaring. Noticing the other pirates stepping from the tents, she forced herself to unclench her fists, then proceeded to walk to the containment units.

Craggy walked past Martin and stood over his full plate of food. The last to be served, Martin Fry had not had his chance to eat yet. Craggy waited until Martin looked over at him, then kicked his plate into the fire. Martin caught his breath and stood up. He locked eyes with Chuck. He could see the young man's anger turning his face red. Martin shook his head slightly. *Don't do anything stupid.*

Gillion approached the campfire. In his hand was a can of rations taken from the shuttle.

"You're pushing your luck, Dr. Fry," he said, his mouth full.

"I suppose I'll get back to welding," Martin said.

"That's the smartest thing you've said all day," Gillion said. As he turned around, he glanced down at Kim. "Since the loader's busted, I might have to find something for you to do." He walked deeper into camp, while Craggy followed Martin to the containment unit.

Kim and Chuck sat alone for a moment. Rarely were they able to rest in peace without being under any watchful eyes and prying ears.

"We can't let them get that uranium," Kim whispered.

"I agree," Chuck said. "But what can we do? They've got all the guns. They're gonna get that stuff on a ship with us or without us."

"Not very optimistic of you," Kim said. Chuck wanted to chuckle. This was a much different Kim than the shaky, teary eyed survey assistant that fumbled at the loader controls.

"More like I'm being realistic. It's not like I'm gonna grab up arms and shoot my way out of this place. There's not really any means of putting an end to this."

"Sure there is," Kim said. She took a sip of her water, making sure no pirates were listening in on their conversation. Chuck's eyes narrowed. She was alluding to something.

"Like what?"

"We sabotage the equipment," Kim said. She was watching the container with intent. Chuck's eyes lit up.

"Did you—" he stopped, leaned in and lowered his voice to barely a whisper, "Did you bust the loader on purpose?" Kim gave a slight nod.

"The containers can't be loaded without the proper equipment. They're too heavy to load by hand, even if twenty pirates tried lifting it. Makes you wonder how they built the damn pyramids." Chuck was flabbergasted. Kim, by her own admission, was clueless about machines.

"How'd you know about the oil and the—"

"When we were nearing the planet, I watched you prep the vehicles," she answered. "You were talking with one of the crew, letting him know which fuel types go with which machines and what could go wrong, yadda-yadda."

Chuck's eyebrows raised. "You were watching *me*?"

Kim realized how she sounded. Even now, as a captive in a pirate camp, when she wasn't sure if she'd live to see the next day, she felt embarrassed for checking out a guy.

"Yeah, that sounded creepy," she said, trying to play it off as a joke.

"Wow," Chuck said. "I'm…genuinely impressed. You paid attention better than most of the diggers." They shared a chuckle.

"I'm an academic," she said. "Maybe not at the level as a graduate student, but it is my job to pay attention to details."

"Did you attend acting school as well?" Chuck asked. "You had everyone fooled over there at the loader. Including myself." Kim smiled, thinking of the kind way he treated her, thinking she was in peril.

"It was an elective," she replied. "Easy course too. Had to maintain that GPA."

Their smiles vanished as they heard Gillion shouting to a couple of his pirates over by the vehicles. He was irate about something, and an irate pirate who already had an itchy trigger finger was nobody to trifle with.

"What do you mean, he hasn't checked in?" Gillion shouted. A pirate holding a high-range comm stammered over his words.

"Rico was supposed to check in thirty minutes ago. We've tried hailing him, but no response."

"And Camp D?"

"Nothing from them either. Nor the patrols. I'm getting nothing from anyone. It's like we're the only ones here," the pirate said. Gillion paced back and forth, deep in thought. The pirates made sure to give him space.

Rico was Gillion's most reliable subordinate. He had traveled into the forest on other occasions and never failed to check in. Gillion wasn't buying that this was a technical issue. One camp failing to check-in? Maybe. All of them? Not so much. Either there was a mass technical issue, or the camps had run into trouble.

Gillion marched across the campsite towards the containment box. Martin and Janet were both standing on ladders, working on welding the patches to the containment unit. Martin's heart thumped as he saw Gillion's hostile expression. He killed his flame and removed his goggles.

"Something wrong, Gillion?" he asked. The pirate leader kicked the foot of the ladder, knocking it over and Martin with it. He fell backward, the ladder landing on top of him. The top step clipped his forehead, drawing blood between his natural wrinkles. Two pirates threw the ladder off of him then lifted him up by the shoulders. Gillion leaned forward, pressing his forehead to Martin's, allowing him to see his angry eyes up close.

"Who did you contact?" Gillion snarled.

"Who? What?" Martin said, playing innocent.

"We've lost contact with all our scouts and campsites. It's no technical failure. Who did you alert? The military?" Martin stammered, unsure of what to say. Admitting he sent a signal would certainly bring harm on either himself or another of his team. Then again, he wasn't good at lying, and if Gillion found out he was lying on top of everything else, then the consequences would be even worse.

One of the pirates approached the leader from behind.

"Gillion? We don't know for sure that anything happened to Rico and the others—" Gillion turned and drew a revolver. A loud *bang* caused Martin to jolt. The pirate reeled backward, trailing smoke from a gaping hole in his chest. Rico looked to the other pirates standing about.

"Anyone else want to offer their opinion?" The question was met with shaking heads. "Good." He pointed his revolver at one of them. The pirate gulped, his eyes going from the muzzle, to Gillion's eyes, and back. "You—" he thought to remember the pirate's name, "Vargo! Until Rico gets back, assuming he even does, you're my new right-hand man." He holstered the revolver. The pirate named Vargo eased himself, though tried to maintain a tough exterior.

"I am honored, Gillion," he said.

"How many perimeter patrols are out?"

"Five," Vargo answered.

"Make sure they keep their eyes open. Have everyone on standby. We might need to make a run for it," Gillion said.

"But what about the merchandise?" Vargo asked.

"What good will it do us if we're caught?" Gillion said. "With that said, I'm getting to the bottom of it right now. You just worry about getting the crew ready." Vargo nodded and moved into the interior of the camp, yelling at all the pirates to gather their gear. Gillion turned around and stared Martin in the eye. The scientist shook his head.

"I've got nothing to tell you," he said. Gillion punched him in the stomach. Martin doubled over, the pirates holding him upright. Gillion punched him again. At this point, Martin was grateful he didn't get lunch: It tasted bad enough going down, he couldn't imagine it the other direction. Gillion grabbed him by the hair and forced him to look up.

"I will ask you one more time." Spit hit Martin's face with each word. "Who did you contact?" Martin sucked in a deep breath and braced for the inevitable blow. Gillion deliberately went low, plowing his fist to the groin. The pirates let him fall to the ground, chuckling as they watched him roll into a fetal position, both hands over his now-blue equipment.

Gillion stood over him. "Still not gonna talk, are ya? That's fine." He looked back and pointed to the young couple sitting by the fire. "Bring the schoolgirl to me."

Kim and Chuck stood up and backed away from the fire. Pirates closed in on them from all sides. Chuck held up his fists.

"Not happening!" he warned the pirates. A few muzzles pointed at him. Chuck didn't care. He charged the one directly in front of him, tackling him to the ground. He hammered a fist into the pirate's nose, landing two blows before a rifle stock struck the back of his head. He rolled over on his back, the world above a blur. The pain, however, was as pure as ever, especially when the pirate he tackled sought retribution. A kick to the ribs made Chuck cry out.

"Stop!" Kim yelled. The pirate proceeded to assault him with more kicks to his side. He drew his knife and knelt down, ready to carve his name into Chuck's skin.

"Not yet," Gillion said. The pirate looked up to him, then sheathed the knife. He stood up and stood guard with two other companions, watching Chuck with loaded rifles. Two other pirates grabbed Kim by the shoulders and forced her over to Gillion.

Gillion drew his knife and held the blade to her throat. Kim trembled, feeling the cold edge press against her skin. Gillion looked back at Martin.

"Don't want to talk? Fine. Have it your way." He moved the knife down and sliced off the top button from her shirt, revealing the golden skin beneath. He moved the knife further down to cut away the next.

"Stop!" Martin shouted. He was on his knees holding his hands out. Gillion removed the knife and stared at him. Martin took in a few breaths, then lowered his hands in shame. "It was me. I sent the call. I didn't receive a response. You had taken over the ship, so I destroyed the receiver." A period of silence followed, after which Martin finally looked up again. Gillion was standing in front of him, the knife sheathed.

"You see how easy that was?" Gillion said.

"None of this has been easy," Martin said.

"You've made it harder than it has to be," Gillion replied. He marched back and grabbed Kim by the back of the neck, then threw her to the ground. "And now, she'll have to pay the price!"

"What? No!" Martin shouted.

Gillion snapped his fingers at the two pirates standing guard. "Have fun, boys. You've earned it." Both men grinned and looked at the frightened girl. Kim shook her head.

"Don't you even—" She kicked at them as they descended down on her. Her screams echoed through the sky. They grabbed at her, trying desperately to get her clothes off. Gillion chuckled, lighting a cigarette as he watched the punishment begin. Martin stood to his feet, only to be knocked back to the ground by the guard behind him. The guard pressed his rifle to the back of his neck, keeping the doctor pinned.

"Don't move. Watch," he said.

Janet spun on the ladder step, ready to jump to Kim's defense. Craggy stepped in front of her and pointed his rifle up at her face.

"Ah-ah-ah," he warned, then winked. *Hopefully I'll get a turn…with you.* He licked his lips at the thought. Janet clenched her teeth in outrage, forced to stand back as the pirates assaulted.

Several yards back, the pirates guarding Chuck had forced him to his knees. One hit him in the groin, killing any fight left in him. The other grabbed him by the hair and forced him to watch, then laughed at their comrades' savage actions.

CHAPTER 7

Sakai kept low. He could see the edge of the forest up ahead. Beyond that was the pirate camp. He counted five perimeter guards moving within the trees. They would have to be dealt with before the team could move in closer.

There was roughly four hundred feet of forest between him and the tree line. The nearest pirate was less than twenty yards away, completely unaware of his presence. The furthest was at the tree line, while the others were wandering in-between.

Sakai had his knife in hand. He crouched low, peeking around the tree just enough to keep from being seen. The pirate looked bored, as most sentries did. He stared out into the woods, sucking on a cigarette that had been burnt to the butt. He eventually moved closer. Then finally, he turned his back.

Sakai moved silently, not even so much as crunching a leaf as he closed in. He cupped a mouth over the pirate's mouth and ran the knife over his throat. The pirate spasmed violently, letting out a muffled gurgle before his body went limp. Sakai dragged him back and ducked behind a row of bushes.

The next nearest pirates heard something. Sakai watched through the brush as they looked back at him, unable to see him. What they did see were branches wavering slightly as if something had brushed by them, and no sign of their comrade. Curious, they moved closer, right into the trap set up by Vance and Ward. Both marines appeared so quickly it was as though they materialized out of nowhere. Both of them grabbed a pirate and sunk their blades into their throats, killing them. Slowly and quietly, they dragged the bodies back behind the trees they hid behind.

Sakai watched the last two sentries. One was still standing at the tree line. Something was going on in camp that had his attention. The other was strolling in from the left side. Sakai heard him calling for one of his buddies, only to receive no reply. So far, the guard at the tree line didn't seem to care, but that could change any second.

"Pharris, respond to his call," Sakai whispered into the comm.

Pinky was fifty feet to his left. He slowly unslung his sniper rifle and placed it to the ground. He held a knife with a seven-inch serrated blade in his right hand. He moved further to the left, waiting several seconds between each tree until he was positioned behind the sentry. He wrapped a hand around the target's mouth and sunk the blade deep, then pulled him down behind a bush. The pirate gurgled then slumped against the dirt, rivers of blood trailing from his mouth and neck.

Pinky held a thumbs up toward Sakai. He couldn't see the Staff Sergeant, but knew he could see him.

"All units move forward," Sakai whispered into the commlink. Slowly, the marines crept up. All eyes were on the final sentry. He was visible from the camp, which meant they had to be extra careful with taking him down quietly. "Pharris, prep your sniper. Bordales and Calloway, use your glasses and get a view of the camp. Let me know if we have any eyes on us while I take out the trash."

Morgan dug for her binoculars. Calloway was fifteen feet ahead of her, army crawling toward the tree line. With her rifle in one hand and the glasses in the other, she slowly moved behind him. Suddenly, she noticed that Calloway had stopped. He raised a fist just high enough for her to see it, signaling to stop. The sentry was starting to turn.

Looks like the bastard finally got bored staring into the distance.

Suddenly, they heard a scream coming from the open plain behind the campsite. Further sounds of commotion followed, as well as laughter. Whatever it was, it was enough to draw the sentry's attention. They noticed a grin come over his face as he raised his binoculars to watch whatever was taking place.

Calloway crawled several yards closer to the tree line, then looked through his binoculars. There was still too much forest obstructing his view, keeping him from seeing what was going on. However, he could see bits of the camp itself. Pirates were walking from their tents, gathering toward the commotion.

"Looks like they're having a party or something, Sarge," he whispered into the comm. "No eyes peering this way, so it seems."

So it seems would have to do. Sakai couldn't wait any longer. There were civilian lives at stake, and on top of that, he had no interest in being in this forest any longer than he had to after seeing what happened to the pirate patrol.

He stood up from his crouched position. The sentry was thirty feet ahead of him. Sakai moved fast. Each footprint was barely audible. Twenty feet to go. Fifteen. The last ten was a sprint. By the time the sentry heard the footsteps behind him, Sakai's arms were bent around his neck. He yanked back, pulling the pirate out of view. He twisted hard to the right. There was a simultaneous squeal and *crack*, and the pirate flopped onto the dirt, lifeless.

The marines assembled at the perimeter, keeping back just enough to remain out of sight. Morgan and Calloway moved further to the right, taking firing positions. Pinky arrived with his sniper rifle and took a spot three yards to Morgan's left. The rest of the marines gathered past the Sergeant's left.

Sakai studied the camp through his binoculars.

"I'm counting seventeen pirates near the tents. Eleven Sinkev rifles, four shotguns, at least a dozen sidearms." He saw the fireplace and a man in his early twenties down on his knees with a gun to his back. Two pirates stood beside him, making him watch something.

The commotion further down grew louder.

"What the hell's going on?" he muttered. He panned right and zoomed in. He saw an enormous steel containment box that stood twelve feet high. There was a woman on a stepladder, facing outward with a blowtorch in her hand. "There's one of the surveyors." He zoomed in further and saw two pirates standing over a man, prodding a rifle into his back.

"Oh, shit," Pinky muttered. "Sarge, you seeing this?" Sakai panned further to the left and saw the two pirates wrestling with a young female.

Morgan tensed as she watched through her binoculars. They hadn't gotten her clothes off yet, though that would change in a few seconds. The sight sparked outrage and shame, as she had traveled with people who weren't much better. Many times did her 'employer' disappear behind closed doors with an unwilling female, and she did nothing to stop it.

"What are we waiting for, Sergeant?" she muttered.

"Until they're clear enough to engage, that's what," Sakai said. "We go out now, those pirates will put bullets in those hostages before we even get close."

Morgan shuttered, unable to take her eyes off the struggle. The girl was in her early twenties. Her button shirt was ripped open entirely, revealing the oil-stained white tank top beneath. One of the pirates went for her waistline. The girl kicked up, catching his chin hard with her heel. As the pirate reeled backward, the girl swung a fist, catching the other in the nose. Free from their grasps, she pushed up to her feet, only to be tackled by the pirate she kicked.

"They will kill her when done," Vance's thick Russian accent filled their earpieces. "These pirates only do this to people they intend to dispose of."

"Pipe down," Sakai said.

"Staff Sergeant!" Morgan said.

"Knock it off, Marine," Sakai hissed.

"We've got to do something," Morgan continued. Sakai exhaled, counted the pirates again, then lowered the binoculars.

"Pharris?"

"Yes, Sarge?" the sniper said. Sakai shouldered his rifle.

"Take those two losers out. Bordales and Calloway, you'll flank right. Landon, Vance, circle to the left. Ward, Cutler, you're on me. Hood, you're gonna get your wish. As soon as Pharris opens fire, send some grenades into the main camp."

"You got it, Sarge," Hood replied.

"Pharris, pick the bastards off as you see fit. Just don't hit me," Sakai said. "Now...let's kill some fucking pirates."

Pinky got up and ran several yards to the right, putting himself in better position to snipe the rapists. He positioned the rifle and adjusted the scope. His laser scan locked onto the two pricks. One was holding the girl down, the other was attempting to undo his own pants. The girl kicked him again, this time catching him in the gut. Pinky grinned.

"You think that hurt, dipshit. Wait till you feel *this*..."

****

A blow to the face flattened Kim, knocking her glasses clean off. Exhaustion and trauma took their toll. She stared upward, seeing a sky that seemed to be spinning clockwise. She was out of energy and fight.

"Wow," Gillion said. "I seem to have lost all respect for you losers. Can't even handle a little girl." The two pirates stood on their knees, their faces bruised and bloodied. They would not let themselves be humiliated any longer. One positioned himself behind her head while the other sat on her legs as he attempted to undo her belt for the third time.

He sucked in a deep breath to dull the pain in his gut. "You're gonna regret that, you little bitch," he said. He smiled, baring brown teeth at her. All of a sudden, pain in his gut returned, sparked by an invisible force that sent him reeling backward. Blood exploded from his abdomen and back.

By the time he heard the crack that launched the bullet, his body had broken in two.

The other pirate stood up. It was too late. Another shot rang out, sending a round slicing through his neckline. He was dead before he hit the ground. The pirates dispersed, confused and alarmed.

"Gunshot!" one yelled out.

"Where the hell did it come from?" Vargo asked.

"The trees! You idiots!" Gillion shouted. "They're in the fucking—" A series of explosions tore through the camp, engulfing several pirates and tents. Burning debris hurled through the air, the shockwaves rippling beneath their feet. Another blast erupted, sending two pirates airborne. Every time Gillion tried to shout orders, his voice would be drowned out by another blast, as well as the screams of the men caught in its proximity.

****

Sakai was the first to storm the camp. He sprinted from the trees and quickly found himself in a world of fire and smoke. Twenty feet ahead of him were the first group of tents—what was left of them. Two pirates stumbled from the ruins and saw him. Sakai let loose several rounds in bursts of three, cutting both pirates square in the chest. The explosive tip rounds tore them open and propelled them backwards.

The Staff Sergeant pushed forward, followed closely by Cutler and Ward. They spread out and engaged another small gathering of pirates. Bullets ravaged the enemy, sending rivers of blood into the burning camp.

Morgan and Calloway converged on the south end of the camp, the redneck blasting from the hip. As unconventional as his technique was, he made it work, catching one pirate right in the neck. The explosive rounds ripped his throat wide open, nearly taking his head clean off. Another pirate came into view. Calloway shot off another few rounds, striking him in the chest. The pirate spun, his spasming hand blasting his rifle aimlessly to the sky as he fell.

"Yee-hah!" he exclaimed. He heard the crack from Pinky's sniper rifle and the whistling of its bullet streaking past him. It found its destination in the forehead of an advancing pirate. Blood and brains exploded in all directions, leaving a headless pirate twitching momentarily before collapsing.

Morgan looked back and forth in search of any targets. She saw Sakai racing between the tents. He fired two bursts into another pirate, his bullets creating several pink clouds. As the target fell in a pool of his own blood, Sakai turned to the right. Another pirate was pushing himself off the ground, having been knocked down by one of Hood's grenades. He righted himself and drew his sidearm, then pointed it at the Staff Sergeant. Sakai had already closed the distance. He swept the butt of his rifle to the left, knocking the pistol away, then thrust the stock forward. Its edge caught the pirate right between the eyes, driving him back several feet. Sakai shouldered the rifle and finished him off with a single shot to the head.

"Shit!"

Morgan heard Calloway curse, then dive into a summersault. She looked to the right. The pirate was twenty feet ahead, the grenade he tossed quickly closing in on her fellow marine. Her mind went into the split-second debate of fight or flight.

She sprinted forward and kicked as hard as she could. To her surprise, her foot actually connected with the grenade. It hurtled back in the direction it came, its owner screaming right before it detonated by his head. Shrapnel ravaged his body into an unrecognizable heap of meat. Morgan caught her breath. It was the first direct kill she had ever made. She had conducted suppressive fire in the past and operated gunship cannons, but never had any confirmation.

Automatic gunfire snapped her back into reality. She ducked and rolled to her left. Bullets kicked up dirt where she previously stood. The pirate that fired them moved in from behind a wall of burning debris. He adjusted his aim to fire on her. Morgan unleashed a hail of bullets. The pirated danced in place as red holes exploded in his body. He hit his knees then faceplanted, the ground beneath him turning red.

Already, her second confirmed kill. She was astonished how easy both were. She glanced at her LED reading. She was in the orange now, still containing enough in the mag to keep going.

"Hot damn, girl," Calloway said. "Don't know if you're a regular soccer player, but that was a hell of a goal." Morgan reached out and helped him to his feet.

"Tried out for Division 2," she said.

"Yeah? What happened?" Calloway asked.

"Almost got in…until I kicked a ball right into the goalie's face," she quipped. Calloway laughed, then charged further into the pirate camp.

****

Gillion watched as his dwindling band of pirates descended into madness. Every order he shouted went unheard. It had become every man for himself. Some rushed the marines, only to be cut down by their superior weapons and tactics. Those who fled were picked off by the sniper. He watched one make a mad dash for the shuttle, only for a round to rip through his shoulder, severing his arm. The pirate screamed, watching his blood spurting from the enormous wound before collapsing.

Only four remained close by. He watched the marines closing in, less than a hundred meters from where he stood. Only a half dozen or so pirates remained in the firefight, and he knew they would hold them off a minute or two at best. He glanced back to the shuttle and the Jeeps they had parked in front of it. He then looked at the surveyors. They would need a hostage, but wouldn't have room for all four.

"Grab the women!" Gillion yelled. Craggy grabbed Kim by the shoulders and yanked her up to her feet. He looked up at Janet and reached to grab her off the ladder. Instead, she threw herself down on top of him, knocking him off balance. She swung the torch, clipping him near his eye. Craggy staggered, then readied his rifle.

"You bitch! I'm gonna—"

Janet lit the torch and thrust the shaft in his face, scorching his brow. Craggy screamed and fell backward. Seeing the other pirates closing in from the right, she turned and ran behind the container. Several bullets whizzed past her while others ricocheted from the metal barrier.

Gillion started to run after her but stopped after seeing another pirate hit by marine gunfire. There was no time to give chase. By the time they caught or killed Dr. Saldivar, the marines would have closed in on them.

"Pick her up! Let's go!" he said. Two of the pirates grabbed Kim by the shoulders and dragged her along, while the third pushed Craggy toward the shuttle. Martin Fry stood up, ready to run to her rescue, but like Janet, he was forced to flee as the riflemen pointed their weapons toward him. He ran with the energy of someone half his age, diving behind the container which he had slaved to repair during the last forty-eight hours.

Gillion glanced back. The firefight behind them was coming to an end.

****

"Vance, ten o'clock!" Sakai shouted. Vance saw the pirate taking aim at her. She rotated slightly to the left, lined up her shot, and fired. The pirate doubled over, his rifle sawing the ground in front of him. Blood poured from his stomach. Desperate to keep fighting, he tried raising the gun again. Vance fired again, ravaging the top of his skull.

"Nice try," she said. She heard an engine starting up.

"Up ahead!" Landon pointed. "They're making a go!" A Jeep carrying three pirates tore through the smoke, going north. Its tires shredded tarp as it raced through the camp. Sakai saw it coming right for him. He dived out of the way, feeling the rush of air behind him as it passed by.

He rolled to his knees and fired. Bullets peppered the bumper and exploded the rear-left tire. Landon, Vance, and Cutler unleashed a devastating volley. Bullets tore through the windows, splattering the interior with the blood of the three occupants.

As the vehicle slowed to coasting speed, Hood dashed from the forest and aimed his grenade launcher. Two shots struck the vehicle, the explosions igniting the fuel tank, causing a secondary explosion that reduced the Jeep into a series of flaming debris. The squad looked back at Hood, who cracked a nervous smile.

"Yeah, okay…might've gone a little overboard."

"You think?" Cutler replied.

"Pay attention, Marines!" Sakai said. They swept through the main camp. There was no more resistance. The young man was face down near the firepit, bruised, but otherwise okay. He looked toward the container and saw Dr. Fry and Dr. Saldivar. Only one of the four wasn't present.

"Sarge!" Calloway yelled out. He and Morgan were pointing at the shuttle. Sakai raised his binoculars. He saw the last group of pirates mounting their escape. Three of them packed into the Jeep with the hostage, the other two mounted motorcycles.

"Pharris, can you get a shot?!"

"Negative, not with the hostage!"

"Shit!" Sakai said.

"Over here, sir!" It was Morgan's voice. Sakai looked to the southeast corner of the camp and saw her standing near a Jeep. She opened the door and started the engine. Sakai sprinted to the vehicle and hopped into the back, then smashed the skylight off the roof.

"Marines, secure the area and tend to the civilians," he shouted. "Bordales and I are going after them!"

"What about the hostage, sir?" Cutler asked.

"She's dead anyway if we don't stop them," Sakai said. He loaded a fresh magazine into his rifle, then placed wind protection goggles over his eyes. "Bordales, get me near those bastards. And don't crash!"

"Yes, sir!" Morgan said. She floored the gas pedal, launching the Jeep like a bullet. The engine roared as they gradually closed the distance on Gillion.

CHAPTER 8

Kim bounced back and forth as the Jeep sped over the plains. The landscape was anything but even. At top speed, the vehicle teetered to-and-fro as it moved over the array of hills and bumps in the ground. The survey assistant felt like dice in a cup being shaken.

She was in the back seat. Gillion was in the front passenger seat, constantly looking back. The driver grunted with each turn of the wheel, as if wrestling an unruly mechanical beast. Craggy was seated to her right. A blackish-red line creased over his eyebrow. Fluid leaked in little rivers down his face. It was clear he was in pain. He held a gun to her temple. However, with the turbulence, he could barely even keep himself upright. The gun wavered, sweeping her body repeatedly.

"Keep her down!" Gillion shouted.

"Where shall I go, Gillion?" the driver asked.

"Away from them!" Gillion shouted. The Jeep came to the top of a small hill, which immediately led to a slope. The Jeep soared off the top as though it were a ramp. All hands leaned back into their seats, experiencing the moment of weightlessness before the vehicle touched down again. It went into a tailspin, grass and dirt shooting from the tires like sawdust from a woodchipper. The driver slowed the vehicle until he regained control.

The two pirates on motorcycles raced to Gillion's window. He lowered it and pointed his finger north.

"Head that way to the ravine," he said. "We'll cut through there, turn west, and make our way to Camp D."

"What if the military's there too?" one of them asked.

"Then we'll use our hostage," Gillion said. "Now go!" The bikers sped ahead. The Jeep driver accelerated to only two-thirds of the previous pace. Gillion glared at him. "What are you doing?"

"The terrain's too rough! I can't maintain control," the driver said. "We go at top speed, we might turn over. Or bust an axle."

"If you drive at this granny-pace, we'll be caught," Gillion said. His face tensed and he pressed his pistol to the pirate's temple. "Floor it. Get us out of here." The pedal touched the mat, the extra boost knocking everyone backward.

Kim leaned forward and hugged her knees, trying to keep herself from rocking too hard. She was already beaten and bruised, and now nausea was being added to the mix. She was starting to see double. It almost appeared she was seeing six pirates instead of three.

Craggy put his hand on the back of her neck, keeping her in place. That, or he was resting against her to keep himself balanced. Regardless, the greasy feel of his fingertips added to her queasiness. Somehow, the sensation helped her to focus on what was happening. There was no fate with these pirates that served in her favor. Even if they kept her alive, it would only be for their sick desires, and in the end, she would be killed and disposed of in some corner of the galaxy, unlikely to be found by civilized humans.

I'd rather die here, she thought. She glanced to the door on her left. All she had to do was pull the lock, open the handle, and dive out. It wasn't a military or prisoner transport vehicle—it wasn't designed to contain people against their will. Any passenger could unlock their door. The challenge was to not get shot, and to avoid getting busted up when getting out. Seeing the landscape whipping by, it was clear that diving out would end up in several broken bones. This far from camp, that was probably a death sentence in itself. She would have to slow them down first, then bail out. If the plan didn't work and she got killed, it was still better than being taken hostage.

She watched Craggy in her peripheral vision. He kept his hand over her neck, though his grip was loose. The gun was six inches from her temple. The Jeep bounced slightly, causing his aim to waver. She took advantage of that moment to glance up at his face. He was squinting, clearly in pain. He wasn't even watching her. Instead, he was staring ahead at the upcoming landscape. They were approaching the ravine. At the end of the plain was a huge gorge full of sand-colored rocks. Kim had seen it before. If she was going to escape, it would have to be now. Diving out on a grass hill was definitely more suitable than rocks.

The Jeep bumped upward, causing the pirate to lean to the right, the pistol momentarily lifting upward. Kim uncoiled and threw both hands at his wrist, shifting his aim to the driver. All three pirates shouted. The gun went off beside the driver's ear, the bullets punching holes in the windshield. His foot lifted from the gas pedal, slowing the vehicle. Kim thrust an elbow into Craggy's nose, knocking him back. She went for the door and unlatched it. A gust of wind embraced her as she opened it and leaned out.

"Stop her!" Gillion shouted.

The nerves in her head lit up as the guard grabbed a fistful of her hair and pulled back. Kim screamed while twisting and throwing her elbows back to free herself. One of her blows struck the pirate in the teeth, loosening two of them. He maintained his grip.

The driver slowed the vehicle to a stop.

"Get back in here you little bitch," Craggy snarled. He leaned forward and wrapped his other arm around her waist, pistol still in hand, and pulled her back in. "Thought you were being clever there, didn't ya?!" He threw her back against the seat and pressed the muzzle to her chin. "We'll have to do something about that, won't we?" His eyes lifted, looking out at the landscape behind them. His snarling expression turned into one of pure fright. "Boss! Look!"

Gillion turned and saw the Jeep racing after them. One thing was for sure, there were no pirates inside of it.

"Shit! Floor it! Go! Go!"

Tires sliced the ground like rubber chainsaws, propelling the vehicle toward the ravine. Gillion checked his magazine then opened his window to shoot at the pursuers. Meanwhile, Craggy slammed a fist into Kim's temple. She fell to her left, leaning against the door. She was conscious, but heavily dazed.

"Don't you move," he threatened, holstering his pistol. He grabbed his rifle and pulled back on the cocking mechanism, then lowered his window to shoot at the marines.

"Keep going," Sakai said. Morgan kept her foot on the accelerator. The enemy Jeep seemed to grow larger as they drew near. They had seen Kim's escape attempt, which served to pinpoint where she was seated so Sakai could properly aim. They were a thousand feet and closing. "Keep it as steady as you can."

Gillion's Jeep turned right and raced toward the ravine. From high above, it looked like a series of enormous cracks in the earth. Cliff edges overlooked the deep gorges that traveled beneath it. The pirates hooked further to the right. Sakai studied their trajectory and the landscape ahead of them, spotting their destination. There was a relatively clear incline between two cliffs that led to a path through the gorge.

Something came out of it and raced past the Jeep. The bikers.

"Keep it straight," he told Morgan. He gazed down the rifle sights. The bikers were not the brightest. Coming straight toward him like this, they were unknowingly lining themselves for the kill. They traveled parallel, twenty meters apart from each other. As they closed in to five-hundred feet, Sakai could see the pistols in their hands. He aimed at the pirate on the right and fired. A pink cloud burst from the target's head and he fell sideways, the bike wobbling back and forth before smashing along the hillside.

The other biker veered sharply to his right, firing aimlessly at the marines' general direction. He then tried to hook back to the left in an attempt to throw off Sakai's aim. Morgan cut the wheel to the left and floored the accelerator. In five seconds, her grill was within a hundred feet of the biker, staring him right in the face.

Sakai fired. Explosive-tipped rounds popped holes in the pirate's chest. He flipped backwards, his bike speeding to the side.

"Nice work, Marine," Sakai said.

"Thank you, sir," she replied. Hopefully, she didn't sound as flustered as she felt. The compliment was genuine, something she wasn't used to from the Staff Sergeant. Of course, it didn't take long for her to screw up again. She looked ahead in search of the enemy vehicle. "Sir, I've lost eyes on the target."

"Two o'clock," Sakai said. The irritation had returned. She cut the wheel and sped toward a large cliff wall. She saw the large crack down the center, roughly twenty feet wide. Just as she saw it, she spotted the enemy Jeep disappearing into the opening.

Morgan lined her vehicle up with the gorge. Instinct and fear roared in her mind in an attempt to get her to slow down. She didn't. They entered the gorge, momentarily going airborne after passing over a small rock ledge. They landed on smooth ground—relatively smooth. She weaved past several boulders, her commanding officer thumping against the edges of the open sunroof.

"Twelve o'clock," he said. The pirates were only a couple hundred feet away. Unlike Morgan, they *did* slow down upon entering. And despite this, they still managed to bump into several rocks. The grill was scraping the ground. The driver's side was dented in and covered in grit.

Craggy thrust his upper body out of the rear right window and pointed a rifle toward them. A three-round burst from Sakai's rifle ravaged his neckline, exploding out the back of his neck. The pirate let out a brief yell then fell, his body hanging halfway out the window. The Jeep veered right to avoid another boulder, causing them to sideswipe the cliff wall. They scraped against it for over a hundred feet, smearing Craggy's body the entire way until he fell out completely.

The driver cut the wheel to the left, nearly driving right into another boulder. Morgan followed closely, bouncing in her seat as she sped over the disproportionate terrain.

Sakai kept his sights on the back window. He tried to center on the driver but could not get a clear shot without putting the hostage in danger. He panned slightly to the right as Gillion extended his torso out the window to fire at him. The pirate leader's eyes went wide as he saw the rifle already pointed at him, then ducked back in.

Unable to get a clear shot, he aimed down and fired a shot into the rear right tire. The hub cap shot out to the side like a torpedo, launched by an explosion of rubber. The vehicle wobbled heavily then veered to the right, putting the front passenger tire in Sakai's aim. Explosive rounds punctured the tire and ignited. Shreds of rubber flew to the side, along with fragments of ball joints and steering knuckle.

Morgan hit the brake, putting distance between themselves and the pirates as they slammed into the cliff wall. The driver tried to cut back to the left, only to smash the bumper against a line of two-foot rocks. The Jeep flipped forward and landed on its back, its remaining tires still spinning. The vehicle spun like a top, completing nearly two full rotations before settling.

"Pull over thirty degrees left," Sakai said. Morgan veered then came to a screeching stop. Both marines then tore out of the vehicle at once, rifles pointed at the Jeep. The passenger side was facing them. They could hear movement from within. Glass from the windshield littered the ground under the hood. A door opened on the other side. "Check your target before you fire," Sakai reminded her. Morgan steadied her breathing.

They heard someone fall on the other side of the vehicle. Both marines fanned out, with Sakai watching the engine side. Stumbling into view was the hostage.

Kim stumbled, dazed from the crash.

"Run this way!" Sakai shouted to her. Kim looked over and saw him. As she started to run, another figure sprang into view behind her.

"Not so fast!" Gillion snarled. He reached out and wrapped his arm around Kim's neck, pulling her backward. He pressed his pistol to her head.

Sakai and Morgan stood firm. They could see the second pirate peering around the rear of the upside-down Jeep.

"Give it up, Gillion," Sakai said.

"Throw your weapons down, Marines," Gillion demanded. Sakai shook his head.

"Not gonna happen," Sakai said. "Give up now. Let the girl go, then turn around with your hands behind your head. Better to be in prison than dead, isn't it?"

"Why don't you ask her?" Gillion said, shaking Kim. His arm tightened, nearly cutting off her airway.

"You're not taking her," Morgan said.

"Oh really?" Gillion snarled.

"Let me get this out of the way—there's no version of this confrontation where you win. You put a bullet in her, you'll only have two seconds to relish it because we'll tear you apart."

"Nice try, Mr. Marine, but I know your rules wouldn't allow that," Gillion challenged.

"Depends on who we're dealing with," Sakai said. "Luckily, we're dealing with pirates, so it's my discretion—and I'm smart enough to know that if she leaves with you, she's as good as dead."

A few seconds of silence followed. Gillion felt himself starting to shake. The marines called his bluff. He had no reservations about killing the woman other than it would simply lead to his death. He was no religious extremist with the promise of a glorious afterlife, nor was he a soldier who was willing to lay down his life for his convictions. He was a pirate, plain and simple, who lived for the here-and-now. All he wanted was gold, money, women, and power. Death gave him none of those, and this bastard marine knew it.

Still, he couldn't let himself be captured. The Death Penalty was a common sentence for pirates, especially captains who usually rose to position after years of heinous crimes and murders. There were plenty of those charges in the recent hijacking alone, not to mention all the other things he had done in the years prior.

He glanced over at his driver, who was looking back at him, awaiting instructions. He was crouched near the rear of the Jeep with his rifle held close to his chest. His legs were twitching. He was eager to run or fight, but he certainly didn't want to stay here.

There was something else, something beyond him. Movement. Whatever it was, it blended in with the rocks. The driver noticed his captain staring past him. Suddenly, Gillion's eyes widened. A gasp escaped his lungs.

The driver looked the other way and saw the beast crouched atop a boulder. Its head was pointed like a spear. Two eyes stared at him with catlike pupils. The gums peeled back, revealing curved teeth. Its legs bent, its arms ready to lash out. In this crouched position, it was almost as tall as a man. Had it been on level ground and standing straight, it would stand a head taller than him.

With an ear-piercing screech, it sprang. Claws and teeth tore into the pirate, spraying his blood across the vehicle.

"What the hell?" Morgan said, stepping back. She only caught a glimpse of its reptilian shape before it dove behind the Jeep. All she could see now was its whip-like tail thrashing about. The pirate screamed, his blood splattering the cliff wall.

Gillion staggered away, his eyes switching between the beast and the marines. Kim tried to scream, but her breath couldn't get through the chokehold. She gritted her teeth in fright, watching flesh being torn from the pirate in large strips.

Sakai sidestepped, keeping his weapon on Gillion. Even he was conflicted on what to do at this moment: deal with Gillion or the creature? In a split-second, he reminded himself to focus on the objective, which was to rescue the hostage.

"Give up now—" Movement caught his eye. One of the creatures was perched on a rock ledge, staring down directly at the pirate captain. It was the first time since his rookie year he questioned his senses. It was a true-to-life dinosaur, here on an alien planet.

Gillion felt its drool rain down on his neck. He looked back just in time to see the array of teeth and claws descend on him. The creature landed on his shoulders, knocking him to the ground. Kim fell from its grip and hit the ground. Less than a yard to her left was Gillion. He screamed as the creature plunged one of its eight-inch claws into his upper back. Like a dog scraping dirt with its hind legs, it raked the claw down his back, shredding the flesh. Agonizing screams filled her ears as she jumped to her feet and ran.

Sakai ran to greet her and help her into the Jeep. As she dove in, he noticed more movement in the interior of the ravine. There were at least six or seven other creatures, leaping over boulders and ledges…coming straight at them.

Gillion let out one final scream as the beast closed its jaws around his neck. Teeth sank in from both sides, ravaging his windpipe and jugular vein, before ultimately scraping against the neckbone. Gillion spasmed one last time before slumping dead against the rock floor. The creature stood straight and laid eyes on its next target.

"Look out Sarge!" Morgan screamed. Sakai glanced over his shoulder and saw the creature moving toward him at bullet speed, arms outstretched, bloodstained jaws wide open. Rifle cracks filled the air and suddenly the creature was knocked to the side, shrieking in pain. It fell on its side, its right shoulder blown open by rifle rounds. Morgan rushed to the vehicle, her muzzle trailing smoke. Its tail thrashed as the creature righted itself. Sakai shouldered his rifle and fired a burst into its head, blowing out a mix of tissue and bone. The creature fell back down, jaw slack, in a mix of blood and froth.

"Let's go! Move! Get in the damn Jeep!" Sakai yelled. The marines hurried into their seats. Luckily, Morgan left the engine running. The creatures were less than a dozen yards away. She put the vehicle in gear, spun the steering wheel to the right, and floored it, performing a tight U-turn. The creatures raced into a full sprint, keeping pace with the Jeep as Morgan sped out of the ravine. She zig-zagged, dodging the very same boulders that hindered their arrival.

The raptors easily maneuvered through the gorge, hopping over any boulder in their path. With feet designed to run over uneven terrain, they quickly closed in on the Jeep.

Sakai watched the mirror, seeing one coming up along his side. He drew his pistol and aimed it out his window. The raptor saw him and roared, spurred by the sight of fresh meat. He squeezed the trigger repeatedly, putting several rounds in its neck. It roared again, this time spouting blood. It slowed down and staggered. Suddenly, several pack members descended on it, wrestling their companion to the ground and shredding its flesh with their claws.

Two others continued chasing the Jeep all the way to the end of the gorge. Sakai reloaded his pistol and waited until another one closed in. As it came within ten feet, he leaned out the window and aimed. The creature saw the weapon, then suddenly dashed to the right. Sakai's shots went wide. He ducked back into the vehicle.

Morgan sped the Jeep up the incline and out of the gorge. Now on better ground, she pushed the vehicle to its top speed. The two raptors continued chasing, roaring in frustration as their prey gradually gained distance. Finally, after nearly a minute of pursuit, they gave up.

Sakai watched the rear-view mirror until he was assured the chase was over. "Now we know what took out that pirate patrol." He looked back at Kim. "Hey, ma'am. I'm Staff Sergeant Akira Sakai and this is Private Morgan Bordales with the U.W.O. Marine Corps. Are you injured?"

Kim was still trying to catch her breath, her mind overwhelmed with the series of events that occurred in the last half-hour. She fixed her shirt and sat up to buckle herself in properly.

"I'll live," she said. "Just, *please*, get me off this fucking planet."

"Believe me, that's next on our agenda," Sakai said. He sat straight and checked his ammo. His rifle was still in the green. He glanced over at Morgan, grateful and surprised she had the reflexes to hit that raptor before it got to him. "Thanks for the save," he said. Morgan looked at him, momentarily confused, then smiled when she realized what he was referring to. The last few minutes had been so chaotic, she had already forgotten. Sakai's grateful expression transformed back into its usual stern one. "Eyes on the road, Private."

"Oh! Right," she said.

"What the hell were those things?" Kim asked. Both Morgan and Sakai felt foolish to admit what they saw. Had they heard anyone else describe those creatures, they'd think that person had lost their minds. But it was true, they were real.

"Damn...dinosaurs," Sakai said.

"Raptors," Morgan added. Everyone was silent. "Let's be honest...we ALL had dinosaur toys growing up."

"One thing's for sure, they're not extinct here," Sakai said. Kim shook her head.

"But there was a scan done on this planet. Nothing in the initial survey showed these things."

"Well, we can go with your scan, or we can go with what we just saw back there," Sakai said. "One thing's for sure: we're getting off this planet."

"What about our construction team?" Kim said. "The pirates had a camp at Mt. Dragoon up in the northwest ridge."

"We'll come up with a game plan, miss, but for now, I have to get you people and my team off this planet. You saw how those things move and how they rely on numbers to overwhelm. We're not equipped, or knowledgeable enough, to handle these things. There's no telling how many of them there are. Going through the forest will be like ringing the dinner bell."

"They're sneaky too," Morgan said.

"And smart. They've learned our guns can hurt them," Sakai said. He activated his commlink. "Sakai to Pharris."

"I hear ya, Sarge!"

"We've secured the hostage. Get everyone ready to depart. We'll be leaving in a hurry."

"Pirate reinforcements?"

"Negative. I'll explain when we get there. Get Ward on the Comm."

A moment passed.

"Ward here."

"Ward, use the remote-control unit to fly the ship to your location. Again, I'll explain in detail when we arrive, but to put in perspective...the pirate traces we found...we figured out what happened to them. Keep your eyes open. And stay the fuck away from the trees. See you in five. Sakai out."

CHAPTER 9

"What the hell's going on?" Ward said to himself. He knelt by his portable terminal, watching two small monitors. One displayed aerial cam footage, the other showed a radar image of their location and that of the dropship. The aerial one shook repeatedly, as though something was pummeling the ship.

"Is it still happening?" Pinky asked him.

"Yeah," Ward said. "Right as I took off. Of course, they make these stupid terminals so cheap, so I can only access one security feed at a time." The camera view dipped again. "Agh! Right there! Something hit the ship." He was getting annoyed.

"Well, you are flying low," Pinky said.

"I'm not bumping into any trees, Corporal," Ward said. He maneuvered the ship remotely, catching glimpses of vague shapes in the corners of the monitor. "Probably birds." He activated flares. It seemed to work.

"Would've been big birds," Pinky said.

"There's a thousand registered planets. It's not unreasonable for one of them to have oversized birds," Ward said.

"If you say so," Pinky said. He stepped away and allowed the pilot to work. Over by the campfire, Cutler was tending to the civilians. Martin and Janet were seated together on one of the logs, while Chuck stood, impatiently watching the distance for Kim's return.

"You sure you don't have any other injuries?" Cutler asked as he prepared some disinfectant.

"Nothing that won't heal on its own," she answered. Cutler touched the disinfectant to one of her many scrapes. "Ow!" She leaned away instinctively.

"Ah-ah, no-no, get back here," Cutler said. He put a hand on her shoulder and tilted her back. "You know just as well as I do that you could easily catch some kind of infection."

"Yeah, I know. It just stings like freaking hell!" she said. She was sitting at the campfire, surrounded by the ruins of camp. Pirate corpses were everywhere. Never had she seen so much death at once. She looked over to the left and saw one pirate on the ground, arched backward, his eyes pointed straight at the camp. Cutler followed her gaze, saw the body, then looked back at her again.

"We'll get you out of here shortly," he said. "I imagine you're probably not used to being around a bunch of dead bodies."

"Not like this," she said. "But I'm no stranger to death. I've seen some bad accidents. I'm a geologist and I'm always on digs. Sometimes there are accidents, especially when you're working around big rocks."

"Nothing like *Indiana Jones*, I hope," Cutler said. He finished applying the disinfectant and tied a couple of small bandages to her arm. Janet smiled.

"No, not quite like that," she said. Up ahead, Chuck was pacing back and forth, impatiently watching the north plains. He was slightly hunched over from being struck in the gut by the pirates. "Chuck, why don't you let the medic take a look at you."

"I'm fine," Chuck said, his voice cracking from the gut pain. Twenty feet to his right was Ward, shaking his head as he remote-piloted the ship.

"We already told ya, kid. Your girlfriend's safe. The boss told us so," he said.

"She's not my girlfriend," Chuck said.

Ward laughed. "Yeah! Right! You're doing a great job of convincing me of that with your immense concern for her well-being. Either you two are a thing, or Ms. Survey Lady has a stalker on her hands." A few marines chuckled.

Martin Fry walked up to Chuck and tapped him on the shoulder.

"Chuck, it's fine," he said. He sounded like a father guiding his son. "Everyone knows there's something there between you two."

"Dr. Fry...really, there's nothing going on—"

"Well in that case—" Ward interrupted, "that means she's available!" Chuck whipped toward him, his face tense with jealousy. Ward pointed and laughed. "Ah! There it is!" The group broke into laughter, including Martin and Janet. Chuck felt foolish for taking the bait. But then again, he was grateful he did. It made him realize that those feelings he'd tried to suppress were real, and not just something that happened when one spent too much time away from home. He smiled and embraced the levity with the others.

"How long till that dropship gets here?" Pinky said.

"Just another minute or two," Ward said.

"What about the team members from the dig site?" Martin asked.

"We'll get you guys off planet first, then make a plan to rescue them," Pinky answered.

"Wait…you haven't rescued them already?"

"No," Pinky said. "This camp here is the first group of pirates we've encountered."

"Huh?" the three surveyors exclaimed.

"We thought you'd hit their other sites," Janet said. The marines gave questioning looks, not understanding why she thought that. Martin saw this and stepped in to elaborate.

"Gillion lost contact with his other camps. From what we heard, they've not heard from anybody. They sent a team out, but they haven't checked-in either. I thought you guys neutralized them first before coming here."

"Negative. We haven't hit those sites. Not yet, at least," Pinky replied.

"Why not go after them now?" Chuck asked.

"Staff Sergeant Sakai has discovered a new threat and has ordered that we get you off the planet first, then evaluate the situation before we make a second rescue attempt."

"Not very conducive to engage enemy personnel while babysitting civilians anyway," Calloway said, spitting tobacco with every other word.

"I don't get it," Chuck said. "Why did they send just the nine of you? Shouldn't they have sent a whole battalion?"

"Sorry, bud, but we were the only ones in the quadrant when your call came in. Other ships are on the way, but seeing as far out as you are, they might take another day or two," Pinky explained.

"You're lucky to be alive as it is," Hood shouted from the trees. He rubbed cleaner over his grenade launcher.

"Marine, you were ordered to stay away from the trees," Pinky shouted.

"My bad, Corporal," Hood said. He walked through the battered tents, brushing by Vance and Landon along the way as they stood guard. He passed the campfire and gazed at the containment unit. "As I said, you're lucky to be alive. Not quite in the nature of pirates to keep prisoners. Something tells me it has something to do with that thing." He pointed at the box. "What were you guys *really* doing here?"

"Can this wait? The Sarge is almost here," Pinky said. They could see the Jeep moving into view. The roaring engine sounded as though it was much closer. Morgan had the pedal to the metal. It was clear that Sakai was in a hurry to get off this planet. And if Sakai was eager to leave, then it definitely was something serious.

Hood stepped in front of Martin and Janet, his boots kicking over the few embers left on the campfire.

"What's going on here? This wasn't a simple loot," he said. Martin took a breath.

"During the first survey, our scanners detected a vast uranium deposit in Mount Dragoon," he said. "Our expedition was to recover some of it and transport it to a holding facility on Petram."

"Why hire geologists to transport uranium?" Ward asked.

"She's a geologist. I'm not," Martin said. "I'm a nuclear physicist. These containers contain shields to protect against radioactivity. More ships were due to arrive, but luckily they retrieved my signal, as your ship did."

"I think we have bigger things to worry about than uranium," Pinky said as the Jeep sped into camp. Sakai was already out the door before it came to a stop. He marched over to Ward.

"Christ, Ward, what's the goddamn ETA?" he said.

"It's almost here, Sarge," Ward said. "I don't know what happened. There was interference of some kind."

"Magnetic?"

"No. Physical. I nearly lost control twice. It was as though something was impacting the hull. I didn't see anything on camera," Ward said. He realized Sakai was still waiting on an answer regarding the ETA. "Thirty seconds, Sarge."

"Good," Sakai said. "Everyone get ready to board." Morgan helped Kim out of the Jeep. Chuck quickly rushed over to her.

"You okay?"

"I'm fine," she answered. The rest of the marines hustled into the open plain.

"What's the update, Sarge?" Pinky asked. There was slight hesitation in Sakai's answer. He knew he was going to sound crazy but there was no time to mince words.

"There's dangerous wildlife on this planet," he said. "They killed Gillion. Nearly got us too. They're—enormous reptiles…"

"Like Komodo dragons?" Cutler asked.

"No, more like—dinosaurs," Sakai said.

"Hold on, what?!" Ward said.

"Dinosaurs? What, is this Triassic Planet, or something?" Hood remarked.

"It's true!" Morgan said. "I saw them too."

"So did I," Kim said. She turned toward Janet. "Dr. Saldivar, it's true. I saw them. One was right next to me." The entire group, marines and civilians, stared in fascination.

"What kind?" Janet asked.

"Raptors," Sakai said. "Don't ask me about the subgroups or subspecies, I don't know any of that crap other than what I've seen in old movies. What I do know is that they're big. They're mean, fast, stealthy, and hunt in packs. Very hard to hit. The only reason we got out alive was because we were in an open enough area. If we go back in those woods, we're dead. Those things can close in on us and we'd never know it until they ambush us. We didn't even see them at the canyon until they attacked."

"We got out of there by the skin of our teeth," Morgan added.

"Probably the only reason we survived this far was because they were too busy feasting on pirates."

Pinky looked at the scientists. "Probably why those pirates lost contact with their camps. Raptors already got them."

"If that's the case, then we're the only ones left on the menu," Sakai said. "Ward, where's that damn ship?!" It was a rare occasion that Ward felt anxious, even when being reprimanded. This was one of those moments.

"It's coming. It's coming," he repeated. Finally, they heard the powerful engines above the canopy. The dropship flew a hundred feet overhead, passing over the group, and gradually landed between them and the large shuttle. Sakai gazed at the eighty-foot ship. There were abrasions all over the hull, like a plastic toy that had been dropped in a thorn bush.

"Those were not there before," Pinky said.

"What the hell could've done that?" Vance asked.

"I don't know, but something was hitting the ship as I was trying to fly it over here," Ward said. "I can only bring up one camera at a time on this terminal. If you'd rather, I could sit here and review the footage—"

"No, I'm good," Landon said. He was the first to run up to it.

"Everyone on the ship now! Go! Go! Go!" Sakai said. Landon opened the loading ramp and hurried into the cockpit. The others filed in behind them. Vance fastened the civilians' harnesses.

"Sorry if that feels tight," she said, pulling the strap on Kim's harness. "But we're taking off in a hurry, which means we're in for a bumpy ride."

"You'll have no arguments from me," Kim replied. Vance finished Janet and Martin's harnesses then took the next seat. Chuck was sitting beside Kim. He felt her clutch his hand.

"Is that too obvious?" she said, jokingly. He smiled and squeezed back. Together, they waited anxiously for takeoff.

Ward went into the cockpit and took a seat next to Landon, who had already initiated the flight sequence. He could hear the engines powering up.

"Whoa, hold up, Trooper! Let me strap myself in. Don't wanna get a ticket for driving without a seatbelt," he said.

"Even now, you can't let the cop jokes go," Landon said.

"Could be worse—with that mustache, we could make porno jokes," Ward said. Landon nodded.

"Yeah—the cop jokes will do."

Ward strapped in and grabbed the controls. "Well then, turn those flashers on and get us the hell out of here!"

Landon activated the comm, "All hands, hope you're strapped in because we'll be taking off in five…four…three…two…" He noticed Ward leaning forward, gazing at the sky. On his face was a combination of awe and terror.

"What the hell is that?!" he said. Landon looked up. A chill went down his spine. In the sky were several winged creatures. They were black in color, gliding like vultures. But these weren't vultures; these were reptiles with a thirty-foot wingspan. Even from high above, their five-foot beaks exhibited menace.

Ward counted over ten of these creatures, all of which were rapidly descending. *Now I know what was causing the interference.*

Landon got on the comm. "Marines, brace yourselves! We've got incoming!"

"Raptors?" Sakai asked.

"No…pterodactyls!"

CHAPTER 10

The flock descended at once, as though they shared a hive mind. In under a second, they swarmed the dropship. Beaks and claws raked over the hull. The viewing glass turned black as wings clapped over it.

Ward activated the forward machine guns. He could not aim—he couldn't see anything. He fired blindly. Cries of pain echoed over the rapid gunfire. A few of the pterodactyls broke off from the cockpit. With visual restored, they applied thrust power. The ship lifted off the ground vertically. Numerous pterodactyls struck the starboard side and clung, causing the ship to dip.

In the cabin, Sakai unstrapped himself and stood up.

"What are you doing?" Morgan asked.

"We can't take off with them all over us. They could damage the thrusters mid-flight." A reverberation of creaking metal traveled through the ship, as if intentionally to make his point. "I'll take the ventral gun. The rest of you, hold tight," he said. He moved to the back and climbed a small ladder, which led into a small space. He hit a switch, activating the turret controls. The circular panel lit up. Monitors came alive, displaying the turret barrel pointing out into a swarm of pterodactyls. They were everywhere, swarming the ship like bees. Beaks pecked at the hull, chipping their tips. The birds continued, unfazed. Like the raptors, they acted as a single pack, or a flock in this case.

He rotated the barrel to stern and saw two pterodactyls perched on the vertical stabilizer. Hearing the rotation, one of the birds turned and pecked at the barrel. Sakai unleashed a barrage of bullets into its torso. The bird screamed as it reeled backwards, its body bursting apart in small pieces.

He turned and fired on the other. Blood spurted from its neck and wings as the bullet stream literally pushed it off the ship.

"Put full power into thrusters," he radioed the pilots.

The ship leveled out and soared ahead. Ward continued firing the forward machine guns, driving away a few birds flying straight ahead. The flock followed it, with several of them slamming into the sides like kamikazes. Some circled the cockpit, searching for a place to get a grasp on the ship.

"Christ, they're keeping up with us," Landon said. "How fast are these things?"

"Not as fast as this," Ward said. He accelerated to full speed. The ship shook as it raced over the landscape and arched skyward. Ward laughed, watching the flock trailing behind in the rear-view monitors. "Ha! See ya, you dumb sons of bitches."

"Bank left! Bank left!" Landon shouted. Ward's laugh came to a sudden end when he saw several flock members directly ahead. He yanked the controls to port but it was too late. The ship and the flock collided, the nose bursting in the ribcages of those unlucky enough to be in the front of the flock. The viewing glass turned into a moving blur of beaks, claws, and wings. A thousand cracks creaked along the panel, which then exploded inward.

Glass scraped the pilot's face as they forced the ship back to earth. Landon gritted his teeth, leaning back in his seat as the birds reached in.

"Sarge! Could use a little help!"

Sakai faced the turret forward, the camera feed flickering due to the heavy turbulence. He shook in his seat, barely able to keep the gun level. He fired a few bursts, catching one pterodactyl right in the face. Its beak broke apart completely, leaving a faceless skull with a tongue flapping loosely. Another burst struck another in the wings, shredding them like tissue paper. The bird screamed as it spiraled to the ground.

The pilots slowed the ship and leveled it out two hundred feet over the ground. The pterodactyls zipped around it like flies, scraping the hull with their claws. Once again, they started body-slamming the sides. Sakai rotated the gun back and forth, trying desperately to repel them. He aimed to starboard and sprayed several dozen rounds into the neck and chest of one that had driven its beak between two panels. As it fell away in a cloud of blood, he saw another one close in.

"Die you mother—"

Before he could fire, another bird struck from behind. Its mouth closed on the barrels and yanked up. The gears groaned as they were moved against their will. Sakai tried to rotate the platform to wrestle the gun free, but the beast refused to let go.

It grasped the shaft with its two-foot claws and flapped its wings. Sparks flickered as the metal components came apart. With a heavy sound that sounded similar to a pistol report, the turret detached completely. The pterodactyl tossed the inedible weapon aside and proceeded to peck at the damaged components within the mount.

Sakai heard its thumping overhead. The ceiling dented inward, then peeled apart like rose petals. Through the breach came the spear-shaped beak, twisting and turning to pry further in. The creature retracted then pressed its eye into the hole. The Staff Sergeant saw the black pupil staring at him. He drew his pistol and pointed the muzzle through the breach.

"See this?"

The following gunshot shredded the eye. The pterodactyl lurched back, screaming in agony. Wind seeped into the breach like an invisible vortex, driving Sakai back to the ladder. He opened the hatch and lowered himself down into the cabin.

The marines tossed back and forth as the ship began to spiral. It ascended suddenly, launching Sakai off his feet. He ducked his head down as he hit the ceiling. A split-second later, he fell back down into the aisle. He crawled desperately to his seat and grabbed the harness. At that moment, his mind registered the wind soaring through the ship. The cockpit had been breached.

"Ward! Landon! You still with us?"

"Yeah!" Ward called back.

"We're not getting out of here!" Landon said. "Too much damage, including a fuel leak! We're gonna have to set down!" Another pterodactyl struck somewhere directly above, forcing the ship to arch downward. There were a series of thuds below. The belly of the ship was scraping against something...many somethings. Sakai glanced out a window and saw that they were traveling along the treetops.

"Pull up!" he said.

"I'm trying!" Ward said. His voice was strained. The birds struck again, driving them further into the trees. "Shit...heads down."

The ship scraped along the treetops. Emergency lights flashed in the cockpit. Alarms of all kinds lit up on the monitors. *Hull Breach. Engine Failure. Fuel Leak. Power reserve failing.*

Ward knew he would have to set down somewhere. He stared ahead, keeping the nose from dipping too deep into the forest. Leaves and debris sprayed in through the broken panel, forcing him to sway back and forth from getting hit in the face.

"Up ahead, twenty degrees to the starboard bow," Landon pointed. Ward squinted, the rush of wind assaulting his senses. They were approaching a mountain range. He could see vegetation on the immense hillside, but it was spacious enough to set the ship down, while providing enough canopy to protect them from the birds. Assuming it would in the first place. He wasn't sure of their hunting patterns and capabilities. Maybe they would just descend beneath the trees and pick them off one after another. The only thing that was certain was that this ship was going to break apart one way or another, and he'd rather be on the ground when that happened.

"Brace yourselves, everyone. We're in for a bumpy landing," he said. "If we survive this, you'll wanna have your guns ready because these things will be on our asses."

He didn't listen for a reply, instead focusing on the mission at hand. The mountain range grew more immense as they approached. The birds struck somewhere on the port side, causing the ship to tilt. Diverting power to the starboard thruster, he corrected the ship, only to get rolled over again.

"Ten thousand meters," Landon said. "Seven thousand. Six...dude, you'll want to slow down...five...four...three...two...Ward!"

Ward hit the reverse stabilizers, rapidly slowing the ship. He steered to starboard, taking them away from the thick forest and over the slope of the mountainside. The constant bumping ceased after clearing the canopy. So far, there were no pterodactyls bombarding the hull. With the rear-view monitors down, he had no idea where the flock was, or if they were even still chasing them.

The alarms continued to wail. The letters for *hull breach* had now turned red. An audio alarm yelled in his ear, *Damage Level Eight.* He switched it off. Damn thing was more annoying than his ex-girlfriend.

He found a section of rock that was relatively clear and level. At least, thirty degrees was more level than anything else he was going to find. He engaged the landing gear. The rear pads extended, the front ones failed.

"Of course!" he said, throwing his hands up. "That'd be too convenient!" Shadows swept over the cockpit. The birds had caught up with them. They chirped, circling the ship. The next moment, many of them nosedived like a hawk chasing a rabbit. They struck directly above, plunging the ship into the mountain. He engaged stabilizers to slow the landing as much as possible, then braced for impact.

The ship struck down directly on the tip of a boulder, which split right through the hull. The cockpit detached and rolled forward, while the remainder of the ship rolled to port. It barreled down the mountainside for several yards before hitting a ledge, settling on its starboard side.

"Everyone out!" Sakai said. He unclipped his harness and caught his seat to keep himself from freefalling. The floor was now as upright as a wall. Marines detached themselves and quickly lowered themselves to the starboard wall. Panels and other components fell loose from the ceiling, hitting a few helmets as they came loose.

Vance unclipped Kim and Chuck and helped them off their seats, while Pinky helped Martin and Janet. The small corridor leading to the cockpit was no longer there. An enormous gap took its place, streaming hot sunlight inside. Two feet struck down right outside of it, turning the light to darkness. The pterodactyl spread its wings triumphantly, then lowered its head to peer inside.

"Let's serve this prick his hors d'oeuvre!" Sakai said. He took firing position beside Vance and Calloway and opened fire on the beast. The pterodactyl staggered back, the bullets popping fleshy holes in its torso. It squealed and flapped its wings, only lifting off a few yards before other pterodactyls descended on it. They drove it down to the mountain. Beaks impaled its back like spears, while claws raked its wings.

Sakai and Calloway ran out through the breach. At their two o'clock, the flock had descended on their own companion. The wounded pterodactyl squawked as flesh was pulled from its back and wings. A couple hundred feet up the mountain behind it was the cockpit.

Three pterodactyls feasted on their sibling, while six others circled overhead. Sakai flipped off the safety latch to his grenade launcher, aimed for the buffet, and fired three times. All three grenades detonated in the center of the gathering, sending wings, guts, beaks, and tidal waves of blood splashing down the mountainside.

There was a series of cries from the creature flying above. The rest of the squad assembled outside and spread out. The remaining pterodactyls saw the prey and started their descent, claws outstretched to grab their prey and race back to the sky.

"Now!" Sakai shouted. The marines blasted a volley, hitting the first pterodactyl. Its poised posture suddenly became a twisted and anguished one. Blood rained down from its many wounds. It spiraled out of control as it changed course, ultimately crashing somewhere out of view. The marines continued firing, hitting the next two. One took an explosive round to the bony crest on the back of its head, ravaging its skull. Wings flapped lifelessly as it plummeted onto the back of the ship, then flopped to the ground. The other took several hits to the legs and belly. It flapped its wings downward, lifting itself back upward.

Hood took position at the front of the team and fired his grenade launcher at the retreating beast. The explosive hit dead center. Both wings shot off its body like arrows, its physique falling several feet back, reduced to a mangled thing spurting blood.

"Yeah-yeah-yeah," he muttered. *Overdid it again.*

The three remaining pterodactyls gained altitude. A thousand yards above the team, they flew in a perfect circle. They screeched to each other, each sound more intense than the last.

"They arguing amongst each other or what?" Cutler remarked.

"They might be, actually," Janet said. She watched the creatures with awe. "Your guns drove them back. But they're hungry and don't want to give up their prey just yet."

"I'll help them make up their minds," Pinky said. He chambered a round in his sniper rifle, found a rock to prop it on, then aimed high. He tracked the creatures, the gun's computer tracking distance, airspeed, temperature, as well as the speed of the target. He selected one of them then tilted his gun slightly to aim in its projected path, then fired.

The pterodactyl flipped over end as the bullet plunged through its shoulder. Its screams echoed over the mountainside as it fell to earth like a meteor, smashing down somewhere far in the distance. Its screams were immediately silenced. The remaining two pterodactyls suddenly descended on their wounded comrade, ready to feast on its remains.

"Nice work, Pharris," Sakai said. The skies were now clear. The flock, aside from the two survivors, had been destroyed. Unfortunately, so had their ship. The fuselage looked like a crumpled soda can. The engines had imploded completely. The thrusters had detached and rolled further down. It appeared the small cargo section was intact.

He gave his team a quick lookover. There were several scrapes and bruises, and it was obvious a few of them were on edge, especially the civilians. However, with all things considered, his marines were in good shape.

"Everyone all right?" he asked. The team nodded. Kim wobbled back and forth, then fainted. Chuck quickly grabbed her and lowered her to the ground, keeping her up against his lap. Cutler opened his supply bag and checked her vitals.

"She'll be alright. The ride was a little much for her," he said.

"Not just her..." Calloway groaned. He staggered behind the ship and vomited out of sight. Hood and Vance chuckled while the civilians gave disgusted expressions. The country boy stepped back into view, wiping the sweat from his brow. "All better."

"Vance, Hood, check the ship and salvage any supplies you can. Work fast. Calloway, you stand guard...and drink some water. You civilians wait here with Cutler. Bordales and Pharris, you two with me. Let's check on Landon and Ward. Let's move."

CHAPTER 11

"Come on, get off," Ward groaned as he sawed his knife over his harness strap. Landon pressed a piece of gauze over his cheek where a shard of glass had sliced him badly. Along with that were other smaller nicks and cuts along his face, though mostly small and insignificant. Keeping one hand pressed to the wound, he found his rifle and slung it over his shoulder.

"You need help?" he asked Ward. He immediately winced. It even hurt to speak.

"I'm fine," Ward said. "Damn harness has the hots for me." He worked the blade along the strap, finally cutting himself loose. He stood up, then staggered, still a bit dazed from the crash. He found his rifle then peeked outside. "Coast is clear. Let's get that ugly face of yours over to Cutler."

"Thanks. I'm deeply moved by your concern," Landon replied. They stepped out through the back and saw the remains.

"Hot damn," Ward muttered. Sakai, Morgan, and Pinky approached.

"You two alright?" Sakai asked.

"Still standing at the moment," Ward replied. He pointed a thumb at Landon, "*Scarface* here is gonna need the doc to give him stitches. Are the flying lizards gone?"

"For now. We're gonna have to move quick," Sakai said.

"What's the plan?" Landon asked, wincing.

"I'm working on that," Sakai said. He looked around to get an idea of the terrain. "Maybe we can find a place to hang tight until backup arrives."

"How long will that be?" Morgan asked.

"I told you on the cruiser, at least seventy-two hours," Sakai answered. "Come on. Let's head back down. Some of the team is gathering supplies from the ship."

****

Calloway took in a few deep breaths, still fighting the stirring feeling of nausea. It tormented him with its coming and going. The flight had shaken his hefty mass back and forth, accidentally causing him to swallow a large wad of chewing tobacco.

He focused on his surroundings in his attempt to control his nausea. He could hear his fellow marines shuffling things around in the fuselage. Vance stepped out, carrying a pack full of MREs.

"These'll have to do," she said. Calloway tilted away. Vance scoffed. "Probably the first time I've ever seen you repelled by food. Even by this shit. If you couldn't handle a little roughness, you should've taken up knitting."

"Hey *comrade*, I can handle most things. A dropship coming down in the middle of gunfire, no problem. Zigzagging over God's green…whatever this planet's called…not so much." Vance chuckled. They heard Kim coughing as she awoke.

"Relax, you're fine," Cutler told her. Kim was groggy at first, then shot to her feet as all the recent memories flooded back. "Whoa! You're alright!"

"We're all here," Janet said. She and Chuck put hands on her shoulders, calming her. Kim took a breath and steadied herself. Cutler gave her some water then heard Sakai calling his name. He was relieved to see Ward and Landon alive, despite the former's annoying immaturity.

"Yes sir?"

"Landon's got a bad cut on his face. Can you give him a quick stitch before we get a move-on?"

"I'm on it," he said.

"How's the supplies coming?" Sakai asked.

Hood stepped out, with a pack of magazines in hand. "Two spare rifles, fully loaded," he answered. "No extra grenade bonds for the launchers though. However…" he reached back, "I do have THIS!" He brandished his rocket launcher. Sakai took it, inspected it, then handed it to Calloway.

"What? Am I a pack mule?" he remarked as he slung it over his back.

"Yes," Sakai answered. He looked down at the MREs. "How much were you able to salvage?"

"Eight boxes. The rest spilled out the back somewhere. Oughta last us a couple days, though," Vance said. "We can stretch it out longer through rationing."

"That should do it for now," Sakai said.

"So, what now?" Janet asked. "We just wait here?"

"No," Sakai said. "Too much exposure here. Plus, we have dead animals lying around. Dead animals are food, and I'm not interested to meet their consumers."

"We could find higher ground," Chuck suggested.

"Normally, I'd agree. But higher ground is *that* way, and those raptors were that way," Sakai said. "We can't be sure where any others are, but I know for a fact we can't go east."

"Can't you bring in another dropship from your cruiser?" Martin asked.

"Transmitter got damaged in the crash," Ward said. "What about your shuttle back at the pirate camp? Is that still operational?"

"No. We barely landed it in one piece," Martin said. "Those pirates hit the engines pretty hard when they hijacked us. They stripped everything out from the cargo hold. They took our loaders, our personnel carrier, everything."

"Great. That means we don't have any way off this stupid planet," Ward remarked.

"Not only that, but we're gonna be on foot the whole way."

"There might be another way," Martin said. "The pirates have a shuttle camp, somewhere to the northwest, a few miles away from Mt. Dragoon. If they've been taken by surprise by the dinosaurs, it's possible there might be a ship still functional."

"Dr. Saldivar, do you have any suggestions? Of all of us here, you probably have the best knowledge of the landscape."

"Considering our options, it's worth a shot to go for the shuttles," she said. "That said, it won't be easy terrain. There's streams and creeks, rolling hills, rocks, thick forest. There's patches of marsh further to the north that we DEFINITELY want to avoid."

"Why? Is there quicksand or something?" Landon asked.

"Stop talking," Cutler said. He tapped Landon on the other cheek and continued to stitch.

"No. Bugs. Big ones. Natural species of this planet," Janet answered. Several marines turned, their faces turning pale.

"Bugs?" Pinky said. He glanced to the Staff Sergeant. "Maybe that's what killed those other camps."

Janet shook her head. "No, they're only dangerous if you wander too close to the marsh. That said, we'll have to pass through narrow ground to get between Mt. Dragoon and there." The information did little to ease the tension. Even Janet felt sick as she spoke about it.

Cutler was shaking his head. "I know it's your call, Sarge, but that sounds like a bad risk. Why the hell did the pirates park all the way over there?"

"That's where they first established a base camp," Martin said. "They've got all kinds of crap stored over there from ships they've looted. They've got guns. Vehicles. Even some mechs. The canopy is sparse, but thick enough over there to help protect the ships from aerial scan."

"Look—" Janet said, "given the information at hand, we don't have many good options. I suggest we try and make our way toward Mt. Dragoon. It's higher ground with few trees. Much easier to protect. We've dug a cave near the uranium site, but there's enough earth in-between to keep us protected from radiation. There should be Geiger counters there, just in case. Additionally, it'll give us a chance to see if any of the crew survived."

"Any clue on how to get there from here?" Sakai asked. Janet studied the horizon. Going north would lead them right toward the last two pterodactyls. Any other direction would lead them into the forest, which Sakai had stated he wanted to avoid.

"There's no good answer," she said frankly. "We can follow these hills northwest. The forest isn't as thick up that way. We might stand a better chance."

Sakai let out an exasperated sigh. The geologist was right; there was no good answer. Any decision would put his team in danger. He dreaded the idea of entering the forest, but had to go with the information at hand. What he knew for sure were that pterodactyls roamed the sky, and the canyon where he and Morgan encountered the raptors was just a little over a mile to the east, making this area completely unsafe.

"No other choice then. We're going that way," he said.

Calloway started feeling nauseous again. "Who knows what the hell else we'll find if we go out there."

"You wanna wait here and be lizard food, Marine?" Pinky said.

"Probably not my first choice," Calloway said. "I'm just thinking of what happened to those patrols."

"Think of it this way," Morgan said, "they were unprepared and unaware. Unlike us. We know what to watch for. We have some knowledge of these things. That gives us a slight advantage." She felt herself shiver. Her words were meant to convince herself as much as everyone else.

"We're going whether you like it or not, Marine," Sakai said. "That said, yes, we'll be in danger. Make no mistake, we'll be watched the whole time. Those things will track us, waiting for someone to wander off from the group, so maintain a tight formation, Marines. Do NOT spread out thin. These raptors are sneaky, as Bordales and I witnessed. Anyone wanders too far, they could pick you off and the rest of us wouldn't know it until it was too late."

"You suddenly a dinosaur expert, Sarge?" Ward joked.

"They're pack hunters. It's not hard to think like a pack hunter, especially when you're in the military. And it's what I'd do," Sakai said.

"He's right," Janet said. All eyes turned to her. "I'm in geology, and part of that is learning about fossils. Everything he's said is concurrent with our present day knowledge of these things. Then again, this is a completely different planet, and there's no telling the differences between these species and the ones that lived in Earth's past. If these are in any way similar to the raptor subgroup, they'll have a large claw on each foot. Earth's species had 'em on the middle toe, but these could be different. They're used mainly for bringing down larger animals but make no mistake, they'll pedal these claws on anything they can get a grasp on."

"Pedal? You mean..." Calloway did a bicycle motion with his hands.

"Yes, they'll drag you away, pin you down, then rake their feet across your belly," she said. For the third time, Calloway was feeling nauseous.

Sakai grabbed one of the spare rifles. "Dr. Fry? You ever fire a gun?" The physicist reluctantly took the weapon, his hands trembling from its intimidating design.

"Hunting rifles. Nothing like this," he admitted.

"I'll make it easy for you," Sakai said. He tilted the weapon and flipped a switch on the receiver. "I've set it to semi-automatic. One squeeze of the trigger will fire one round. I don't want you out there spraying bullets like *Rambo*. The safety is off. You were probably taught basic rifle safety when you took hunting courses. Regardless, I'll remind you—keep it pointed away from anything you don't intend to shoot, and your finger off the trigger until that time comes." He grabbed the other rifle, set it to semi-auto, then handed it to Janet. "Any questions?"

"No...sir," she said. It took her a minute to get used to the feel of the weapon. Like Martin, she had only fired a few lesser rifles in her time. Nothing even close to this monster. Sakai took the two spare pistols, chambered a round, then handed them to Kim and Chuck. He briefly showed them how to properly hold them, then showed them how to flip the safety.

"Did you find any holsters?" he said to Hood.

"I did, fortunately," Hood said. He handed them to the younger civilians, who quickly put them on.

"Hopefully you won't have to use these, but considering our circumstances, I'd rather you civilians be armed," Sakai said.

A distant roar echoed from somewhere beyond the mountain, causing all thirteen people to turn with weapons pointed. Whatever it was, it was out of view, which unnerved the group even more.

"Alright ladies, consider that our warning," Sakai said. "Ward, you're on point. I want civilians in the center of the group. Keep it tight. Let's move."

CHAPTER 12

No two steps were the same during the trek down the mountainside. The ground was like a series of ripples frozen in time. There were small mounds followed by small trenches, each equally a pain to pass over. They continued northwest as planned, trying to keep in the clearing for as long as possible before entering the woods.

The squawks of the surviving pterodactyls rang from the east. The two flyers had taken to the air and were going south. Sakai kept a close eye on them during the journey. From where they were, the creatures looked little black planes gliding against the blue sky. He estimated that they had fed and were no longer hunting. For now, at least.

"Whoa," Ward said. He held up a fist, stopping the group. Sakai hustled to the front and found the marine on one knee, inspecting the ground.

"What's the problem, Ward?" Sakai said. As soon as he finished speaking, he saw it. Tracks. Three-toed tracks, trailing across the mountainside. They were three feet in width, pressing a couple inches into the earth. Whatever made them was bigger than the raptors. Considering the solidity of the ground, the thing had to be very heavy to make these prints.

"This just keeps getting better and better," Ward remarked.

"No shit," Sakai replied. He stood straight and studied the trail. "They seem to be going that way." He pointed to the right. "Maybe if we keep going straight, we'll avoid whatever it is."

"*Whatever it is*...we KNOW what it is, Sarge—only a goddamn T-Rex could make this!" Ward struggled to keep his voice at a whisper. Sakai groaned under his breath then waved at the geologist.

"Dr. Saldivar? May I have your input, please?"

Janet moved ahead. Her attention was partially on the huge firearm in her hands. It took no imagination to know it could cause great damage—in fact, she'd seen it firsthand during the ambush. She kept its muzzle pointed downward, away from her marine protectors as she arrived at the tracks.

"Oh...my..." she muttered.

"Sorry, Miss, but you've been appointed our resident dinosaur expert," Sakai said. "You have any thoughts on these?"

"Uh..." Janet was flabbergasted.

"It's a T-Rex, isn't it?" Ward said.

"Knock it off," Sakai scolded.

"Did I hear you say *T-Rex?*" Calloway muttered, a few feet behind them. Sakai's irritated glare made him shut up and step back.

"Whatever it is, it's at least twenty-feet long," Janet said. "A number of species have a foot design similar to this. Could be a Spinosaurus, T-Rex, Allosaurus, probably something very different. As I've said, this isn't Earth. These species have characteristics of their own. For instance, those pterodactyls are way bigger than what we believe Earth's specimens to be."

"Perhaps we shouldn't go any further," Ward said.

"On the contrary, this is probably motivation for us to keep going," Janet said. "These prints aren't very old. It's probably hunting for food. Hell, you saw those pterodactyls had taken flight. It probably drove them off and took their dinner. You wanna be here if it decides to turn back?"

Sakai shook his head.

"You heard her, ladies. We're not invited to this party. Let's keep going until we make our exit."

Janet backtracked until she rejoined her fellow surveyors. The team walked in unison, their caution heightened as each member passed over the prints.

Morgan Bordales lagged at the back of the group. She felt her hand trembling. She lifted it away from the trigger and took a deep breath to calm her nerves. This thing could likely swallow a person whole if it wanted to. The thought of her last living moments being in a monster's gullet triggered a cold sweat.

She shifted her thoughts to her son Jamie and her desire to see him again. Unfortunately, all that did was worsen her anxiety. There was more to fear than the possibility of a horrible violent death; it was the thought that her relationship with her son would never be restored. He would only know his mother as the drug shipper that she was. Hell, did he even know who she was at this point? Did his father even talk about her? Did he remarry and introduce a new woman into Jamie's life? If so, was she the mother figure that Morgan never was? A wave of jealousy swept through Morgan's mind, which soon turned to depression. If she died here on this planet, would Jamie ever know? Would he even care?

Guilt and self-doubt started to take its toll. She remembered the message ingrained during her counseling sessions: the first step to fixing a problem was acknowledging there was one. Part of that was accepting personal responsibility. She ran the risks, knowing full well what the consequences were. Now, it was her responsibility to fix it. She HAD to get off this planet and win her freedom.

"Bordales?"

She looked up from the prints and saw Corporal Pharris looking back at her. She had lagged too far behind. Without wasting time on words, she jogged to catch up. Even as she fought against it, her imagination went wild with ideas of the giant reptilian. Her eyes scanned the horizon. It was out there somewhere.

Hopefully, it had fed already.

CHAPTER 13

The trees were like titans, casting huge shadows over the team. The trees were spaced out in this section of the forest, increasing their field of view. They were still walking downhill, though the terrain appeared to level off up ahead. Bugs zipped by their faces. Cutler groaned under his breath, swatting a couple of pests away from his face.

His hand nearly caught Vance across the face. She leaned toward him, pale skin red, not just from sunburn.

"Doc...they're not gonna kill ya," she whispered.

"Who knows what diseases these things carry," Cutler whispered back. He stepped to the side to put a little distance between them. They were near the back of the group, with Pinky and Morgan behind them. The civilians were in front of him, with Landon patrolling to their left and Calloway to the right. Ward was still on point, with Sakai and Hood next in line ahead of the surveyors.

They watched each tree carefully. Every breeze carried a sense of dread. Every ripple of a leaf, every sway of a branch, no matter how insignificant, drew eyes. They felt like they had walked right into the lion's den. There was a sense that they were being watched. A few of the marines had weapons pointed upward, ready to spray rounds up into the trees.

In the back of his mind, Sakai wished he had packed a flamethrower. He'd burn down this section of forest and any dinosaur in it. He felt a tickle in the back of his throat. He quietly coughed into his hand, then thought about the planet Rominse and the devastation it had suffered. Would he be any better, even if the goal was to save the lives of his people? It didn't matter, he didn't have the damned flamethrower. He took his mind off the subject.

Hardly a word was spoken for the next thirty minutes. They had ventured nearly three miles into the forest. Feathered birds flapped their wings above. Morgan cringed each time. It felt like the damn things were pretending to be pterodactyls.

Though they were no longer walking downhill, the ground was as uneven as it possibly could be. Hills rolled like ocean waves. The brush thickened, causing the team to wind back and forth to continue northwest.

Calloway munched on his tobacco. His stomach had finally settled, though his feet were starting to hurt now. He took back every complaint he ever had about the personnel carriers and their steel, unpadded seats. He'd kill for one of those right now. Plus, it'd put an extra barrier between himself and whatever was out there beyond those trees.

There was a grinding sound with each chew. A few moments passed, and he realized it wasn't coming from himself. He spit it out and listened. The noise continued. It was like a bunch of twigs being crushed into sawdust.

"Psst!"

The group stopped. Sakai could hear it too. There were footsteps—heavy ones. Whatever was causing them was somewhere beyond a large hill to their three o'clock.

"What is that?" Landon whispered.

"It's that big chap that made those tracks, that's what it is," Hood growled.

"We don't know if it's the same one," Vance said.

"Oh, that makes me feel so much better," Hood replied.

"Will you all shut up?!" Sakai said. The footsteps grew nearer. It was approaching. Small tremors shook their feet. "Hood, be ready with that rocket launcher."

"Thought you'd never ask," the marine said. He took the launcher from Calloway, then knelt to a proper firing position, disengaged the safety levers, then took aim.

"Don't fire until it's fully in sight," Sakai said. Nervous breathing could be heard from the surveyors as Vance and Cutler pushed them to the back of the group. The marines formed firing lines. The trees ahead started to shake. "Ready..." Sakai said.

They saw something emerge. It moved around the hill at a strolling pace. Its skin was an amber color. It walked on four legs instead of two. It walked in the space between a few trees. It wore a bony crest on the back of its head that towered over the rest of its body, with curved spines protruding from its ridge. On its nose was a two-foot horn, like that of a rhino. In its beak-like mouth were ribbon-shaped leaves from the bushes. It turned its head and saw the small biped creatures staring at it.

"Don't shoot," Janet warned. "It's a herbivore."

"Styracosaurus?" Kim asked.

"Definitely no T-Rex," Ward said. All guns remained pointed.

"Lower your weapons," Janet said. "I told you, it's herbivorous."

Hood scoffed. "Yeah? So's a rhinoceros. Doesn't mean it won't charge ya."

"You keep your weapons pointed at it, it might do just that," Janet warned.

"Don't think this thing knows firearms," Calloway said.

"No, but it probably knows basic body language and tension, and you guys are radiating it like the fucking sun."

Hot air blew from the creature's nostrils. Its body tensed, its nose lowering to the ground.

"Lower your weapons," Sakai said. The team reluctantly followed his instructions. The six-thousand-pound creature munched on its vegetation, still watching the humans. Its body was less rigid, no longer feeling threatened. It sniffed curiously. After letting out a small roar, it turned and continued on its path.

A wave of relief washed over the group.

"You think it said 'hi'?" Pinky joked.

"Maybe," Janet replied.

"But where the hell did these things come from?" Martin said. "They weren't here before."

"Probably were already here. Just unseen until now…somehow," Janet replied.

"Well, I think we've had enough surprises," Hood said. He handed the rocket launcher back to Calloway, who slung it over his shoulder. "Docs, how much further?"

"There's a river about a mile or so ahead," Martin said. "It's shallow. We'll have no problem crossing it. We'll be able to see Mount Dragoon from there. After we cross, we'll probably have another two miles to go."

"Alright, sightseeing's over," Sakai said. "Move it, people." The marines got back into formation and resumed patrolling west.

Kim and Chuck continued glancing back at the creature as it wandered around. It was a relief to see a prehistoric beast that wasn't eager to tear her apart. She kept glancing back until it was out of sight.

Calloway, on the other hand, was more amused than fascinated.

"Think we'll find *King Kong* while we're here?"

CHAPTER 14

Sakai was relieved to see that the river was indeed shallow. It was barely more than a stream. As Martin Fry had told them, they could see Mount Dragoon in the valley ahead. They could only partially see it due to the number of trees in the way, but it was there, a giant rock surrounded by wilderness.

The Staff Sergeant watched the river, studying each shoreline carefully. Any source of water served as a place for animals to drink. The shore was covered in a blanket of stones, making it difficult to spot any footprints. The river itself was only about twenty feet wide. The stream splashed against several large rocks spaced throughout. He judged that it was around three feet at its deepest point.

There was a tranquility to this area. It was full of nature. There were birds flying overhead. They could see a few monkeys hanging from a low branch across the river. For a moment, they felt like they were in a nature park. Of course, that feeling went away when they remembered they were trying to avoid encountering real life dinosaurs.

"Come on, ladies. You're not afraid of a little water are ya?" Sakai said.

"As long as there's no crocodiles in it," Ward said.

"No," Janet chuckled. "We haven't discovered any crocodiles or alligators in this region."

"Didn't find any dinosaurs either," Ward replied. He was the first in the water. The water was refreshingly cool, even though he hated the sensation of wet clothes. Oh well—in this heat, he'd dry off in minutes. It wasn't like he wasn't already damp from the excessive sweating. He continued on for a few meters, passing one of the big rocks. The water was past his knees now. Sakai went in next, followed by Hood, Cutler, Vance, surrounding the civilians.

"Watch those trees up ahead," Sakai reminded them. "Don't let your guard down." Calloway, Hood, and Morgan stepped into the water behind the civilians. It was almost as clear as glass. Gravel swirled like little grey ghosts being carried away by the current.

Morgan stumbled as her foot hit something hard. She nearly fell forward but was caught by Calloway.

"Careful there," he said. Morgan found her footing and continued on. She realized that some of the 'small' rocks under the water were actually the tops of large buried ones.

She passed by one of the big ones, momentarily watching the water breaking apart as it passed by it. They were halfway across the river. Ward and Sakai were coming up on the opposite shoreline, just ten feet ahead.

Calloway walked on the left-hand side. As he approached the shore he passed by a series of large rocks. The first had a jagged shape with a dark grey color. The next was more rounded in shape, but with a grey color. Because of this, he couldn't help but notice the next one. Its brown color and crooked shape made it catch his eye. Then he realized its texture—it was more leathery than gravelly.

Right then, the 'rock' stood up, untucking its arms and legs. Water spewed from its nose and mouth as the raptor sprang. Calloway hit the water with a tremendous splash, his rifle shooting off several rounds into the sky.

"Jesus!" Pinky shouted. The damn raptor had actually disguised itself as a rock, held its breath under the water, and waited for them to pass by. The river turned red around it. Teeth and claws ripped into Calloway's neck and shoulders.

"Shoot the damn—"

There was another splash and an ear-piercing shriek. Another raptor burst from the water and made a bounding leap, its feet drawn up under its chest. It came down on Pinky's shoulders and drove him facedown into the water, landing right beside Morgan. Its tail slashed, striking her in the face and knocking her into Hood. Both marines fell facedown, the water thrashing violently behind them.

"Get out of the water!" Sakai shouted. "Come on! Move! Get out!"

The raptor drew down on Pinky, biting his neck and slashing his shoulders. Its toes slashed his body armor, unable to breach. Still biting down on his neck, it slashed its hands repeatedly, until one of its nails found the strap. It ripped through it with ease and yanked the armor off completely, exposing Pinky's back. The toes slashed his back, opening him up from the base of his neck to his tailbone. Bloody air bubbles popped along the surface, driven by Pinky's screams under the water.

The other raptor raised its head. In its jaws was a chunk of flesh and bone from Calloway's midsection. His body armor floated down the stream. It saw Morgan struggling to crawl to shore. With a horrid shriek, it dashed for her.

Sakai fired a hail of bullets, stopping the raptor midway. Red explosions burst along its hide, causing it to roar in agony. Another few rounds struck its belly, spilling its innards into the previously tranquil stream. It staggered backwards and fell.

The other darted down the river with Pinky in tow. Vance and Hood fired a few rounds, missing. They stepped a few feet out for better aim, then stopped. There were three more, coming right at them. Water shook from their hides, having been disguised as rocks for the past few minutes.

Vance started backtracking. "Holy fu—" A roar drowned out her voice. Tree branches fluttered overhead, and a brown shape descended. Vance saw it in the corner of her eye. She spun, firing several rounds blindly as it came down on her. Suddenly she was underwater. Pain surged through her body as several ribs snapped. Pinning her with its weight, the raptor sank its teeth into her left shoulder and shook viciously, while its talons ripped her body armor free.

Gunfire blazed from several rifles, hitting the creature in the back. It squealed, staggering off of her. The marines fired in unison, completely ravaging the entire right side of its body.

Hood chambered his launcher and fired upriver. The grenade landed in the center of the small group of raptors, instantly killing one and causing the other two to dart into the trees.

"Fuck!" he exclaimed. Morgan and Cutler rushed into the water and pulled Vance up. She let out a yell, eyes wide with pain. That yell turned into a cough. Blood seeped from her shoulder and spilled down her uniform. Hood briefly looked for her rifle, but gave up after catching a glimpse of a raptor darting in the woods across the stream. There was no time to search for the rifle or the rocket launcher. He followed his teammates back to the shore.

"We can't stay here! Let's keep moving," Sakai ordered. Cutler tried to press padding against Vance's wound, sparking a scream. The brush moved from up ahead. Sakai didn't wait. He aimed and fired. There was a howling roar, followed by sounds of retreat. He looked at Vance then at Martin and Chuck. "Sorry guys, but I have to put you to use. Grab Vance and help her along. Cutler, you can't be a doctor right now. We need to press on!"

"Five seconds, Sarge," Cutler said. He quickly tied some gauze around Vance's shoulder. She yelled again as he tightened the knot. "Hang in there, Ruth."

"I've been through worse," she groaned. It was a lie but one that her squad appreciated. He noticed some bleeding from her midsection. There was a small laceration, but nothing too terrible. Thanks to the armor, and the team's quick reflexes, the raptor hadn't gotten the chance to slash its big claw across her belly. But her ribs—he estimated at least three were broken. Martin and Chuck stepped alongside her and each put an arm around her shoulders.

Vance bared teeth as they helped her along. Her shoulder stung like hell and her stomach felt as though someone was pressing a sharp stick into it. Cutler stayed at the back of the group, cautiously watching their six.

Morgan took point alongside Sakai. She watched the trees. Nothing could be seen behind those thick branches. A raptor could be perched anywhere, and everyone knew it. Apprehension took a hold on the group, especially the civilians. Sakai noticed the group was starting to slow.

"We gotta keep going, people. We're in deep now," he said. The group increased their pace. It brought to mind the old Churchill phrase 'if you're going through hell, keep going'.

The further they moved from the stream, the more the forest thickened. The trees were taller, their branches fuller. Between them were rocks and bushes. With each step came increased tension. It felt like a noose was being tied around the group. Its grip tightened as she noticed tracks in the ground. They were raptor tracks, fresh ones, going across the dirt and toward a group of trees, only twenty feet to her one o'clock. Their lower branches hung low, the vegetation obscuring anything waiting behind it.

"Hold up," she said. She cocked the lever on her grenade launcher and launched one into the center tree. Leaves and wood splinters rained down, the branches cracking as they swayed. The team could hear something heavy hitting branches on its way down.

With a hard thud, the raptor landed on its back, torn from its perched position by the shockwave. Its hip and side were mangled by shrapnel. Thrashing about, it righted itself, only to be torn apart by a barrage of gunfire. It danced in place as holes exploded along its neck and chest. With a gurgling screech, it hit the ground dead.

Its death didn't provide any sense of reprieve, rather it confirmed the fear that these things could be lurking in any tree. There were hundreds of trees between them and Mt. Dragoon. Thousands. And the raptors could be hiding inside any one of them.

"Fuck this," Hood said. He moved up to the front of the group and pointed his grenade launcher at another group of trees. He let off a couple of shots and watched debris launch from the resulting explosions. No raptors fell from the traps, though they could hear some running deep in the woods, spooked by the blasts.

"Go! Go! Go!" Sakai said. Hood took point. After passing another hundred yards, he saw some faint markings on the base of a tree. Claw marks! He aimed fifteen feet high and shot off another grenade. Huge branches crashed down, along with the raptor that hid within them. It had no sooner landed when a barrage of bullets decimated its body. Blood spurted from each gunshot wound. It thrashed its arms and legs before slowing into a final deathly pose.

Sakai looked back and forth. He could hear raptors running back and forth in the distance. Hood could hear it too.

"Yeah! You better run, you fucking cowards! I'm wise to your act! I'll blow you out of the trees!" He led the charge, holding his grenade launcher in one hand and his submachine gun in the other. He sprayed bullets aimlessly into the forest, trying to deter any carnivores lurking within. The LED on his weapon flashed red. He ejected the mag and reloaded, then proceeded spraying more rounds.

The forest became alive with the chaos of forest critters running for safety. Birds fluttered through the canopy, while primates and small reptiles burrowed themselves in dens.

The team ran for another hundred yards, with Vance grunting with each step. Sakai hated putting her through this torture but there was no other choice. He put it out of his mind and focused on the task. Every few moments they could hear movement. With the additional sounds and chaos, it was impossible to pinpoint where each sound was coming from.

"Look out!" Hood yelled. The group halted. Up ahead was a tree trunk heavily marked by raptor claws. He let his submachine gun hang by its sling and took aim with his grenade launcher, muttering, "Like I said— I'm wise to your act, motherfuckers." He fired two grenades into the tree. The subsequent explosions rocked the forest. One of the grenades had struck the base of a branch, sending a huge segment of canopy crashing down.

He watched the debris come down, his eyes searching for the raptor hiding within. "Come on...where are you—"

Leaves erupted from the brush behind his left shoulder. The raptor burst from hiding and zeroed in on the marine, who had foolishly taken the bait. Its speed made it appear as a distortion to the eyes. Its talons wrapped around Hood in a bearhug, sweeping him off his feet. The raptor never stopped running. With the marine in tow, it darted far into the woods.

Several gasps escaped the group. Kim screamed and covered her mouth, nearly losing her pistol. The creature had moved so fast, it almost seemed the marine had been swept away by a ghost.

"Hood!" Ward shouted. There was a scream somewhere behind the blockade of trees, followed by doglike growling and the sound of a struggle. What came next were the sounds of excruciating pain; grunting, gagging, what someone sounded like when having their guts torn out. Ward shook his head, his eyes blazing like a madman. He started to run in after him. Sakai reached back and grabbed him by the collar, stopping him.

"He's gone!" Sakai yelled in his face. The Staff Sergeant's eyes moved up from the marine to the forest behind him. He heard the steps and saw the brush starting to unveil. "Look out!" He tossed Ward to the side and fired his weapon. He only caught a glimpse of the creature, which immediately turned back, roaring in pain. Sakai waved his people on. "Keep moving!"

There was a moment of hesitation before the group moved on again. Sakai took point. Morgan was directly behind him. Sweat was pouring down her face in thick beads. Her hand quivered beyond control. Hood's screams would be forever embedded in her mind.

They came to the top of a hill. It led down into a creek. The water was barely an inch deep, moving south between small rocks. As Sakai crossed, he noticed something in the mud. Tire tracks. Big ones too, moving left along the creek. There were pieces of brass scattered about. The pirates who operated this vehicle were on the run, likely from the raptors.

Janet saw them too.

"The personnel carrier," she said. "It's the only thing big enough to make these tracks." She looked down the creek. "It might be around here somewhere."

"It might not be," Kim said. "It could be another trap. What if those things are waiting for us down there?"

"We'll take a look," Sakai said. "Watch the tree line. We'll look for no more than a quarter mile. At least we have a decent line of sight." They followed the creek, while closely watching the trees. Water splashed with each step. The tracks continuously went up the hill, as though the driver was attempting to escape the creek.

They followed it around a bend in the creek.

"There!" Janet shouted. A thousand feet ahead of them was the personnel carrier. It was on its side, after a failed attempt to make it out of the creek. The group made a mad dash for it, even Vance despite her injuries.

The personnel carrier was one of the many items stolen by the pirate gang, who used it to ship out the workers to the dig site. The entire left side was covered in blood. The windows were shattered, the rear compartment wide open. Morgan climbed up onto the front wheel and peered into the driver's seat. There was some blood on the door and steering wheel, as well as a few empty cartridges below. The driver had been pulled out and dragged away.

Judging by the tire tracks and the many abrasions in its black hull, a couple of pirates had foolishly tried to use it as a getaway vehicle.

Foolish to think they could race through this terrain—Then again, who are we to judge? Morgan thought.

"Hurry! We can flip it back," Sakai said. Everyone gathered around the backside. All except for Vance, whom Martin and Chuck eased to the ground. It was getting increasingly difficult for her to breathe. Martin unslung his rifle and handed it to her, then lined up with everyone else. Sakai led the count. "One, two, three, lift!"

They pulled as hard as they could. The vehicle came off the ground, its passenger side caked in mud. Several of the group members were unprepared for its immense weight and quickly began to buckle. The sound of their strains and the shaking of the carrier alerted Sakai that they were about to lose their grip.

"Lower. Slowly. Slowly," he said. They gently let the vehicle down and shook their wrists.

They heard rustling leaves to the north. They turned with rifles pointed, only catching a glimpse of the raptor before it darted back into the forest. Ward and Landon fired a few rounds after it in hopes of a lucky shot.

"Gosh, when I get home, I'm gonna go to my parents' house and burn all my childhood dinosaur toys," Landon remarked.

"Hurry up, everybody. Let's do it right this time," Sakai said. Everyone knelt down and got a hold on the truck. "Alright…one, two, three, LIFT!" The group summoned all their strength and pulled up. "Come on!" It tilted higher. There was a moment of shakiness as the group struggled to get it above chest level. They pushed harder, finally overcoming the threshold. Gravity did the rest. The carrier came down on its wheels and rocked back and forth.

Chuck quickly ran into the driver's seat. Luckily, the starter fob was still in the vehicle. He pressed the ignition button. The engine growled and died. He tried again.

"Come on, don't do this," he pleaded. The engine rolled over twice then sparked. "Oh, thank you." He kissed the steering wheel. "Hurry up! Get inside."

Martin and Kim lifted Vance from the mud and assisted her up the ramp. Janet and the rest of the marines began to file in, with Sakai taking the front passenger seat.

"Can you get that ramp up?" he asked.

"I'm trying," Chuck said. He flipped the switch controlling the mechanism. "It's not responding. Probably got damaged when the bastards crashed this thing."

"Nothing we can do about it then. Where does this creek go?" Sakai asked.

"I think it dead ends a half mile south. We'll be better off getting up the hill."

"Then do it. And hurry."

Chuck put it in forward gear and floored the accelerator. The carrier shot forward, making it most of the way up the ten-foot hill. The tires splashed the loose soil, losing traction and momentum.

"All terrain, my ass," Chuck cursed, shifting the wheel back and forth to keep the carrier from flipping over as it slid back down. The edge of the ramp kicked up water and stone. Suddenly, the vehicle came to a dead stop, the ramp jammed against some granite under the stream.

"Damn it," Chuck said. He floored the pedal, scraping the ramp further as he backed a few extra feet. He managed to go far enough to turn around and drive north along the stream. "We might have better luck trying to get up the hill around here." He leaned forward to get a better view.

Suddenly there were eyes staring back at him. The raptor had jumped from the hillside and landed directly on the hood. Chuck screamed and slammed the brakes. The raptor dug its claws into the hood, keeping itself latched. It propped itself on all fours and proceeded to headbutt the glass. Cracks shot along the panel. It struck again, sending little shards past his face. It reared back to hit again. Chuck gasped.

Sakai's hand struck him in the chest, forcing him as far back as possible. He thrust his rifle to the glass and squeezed the trigger right as the raptor leaned in. Its skull burst into a fountain of skull, skin, and brains.

"Floor it!" Sakai said. Chuck was frozen, his eyes locked on the reptilian's body and the bullet holes. His ears rang from the deafening gunshot. In this warped state, he never saw the second raptor closing in from his left until its snout came in through the broken window. Its jaws clamped down on his arm and pulled back, sawing the skin and muscle tissue. The creature pulled back hard to drag him out, hitting his head against the frame.

Chuck yelled again as it shook him side-to-side. The meat of his arm tore with each movement. Sakai tried aiming his rifle, but could not get a shot with Chuck being thrashed about in front of him. He dropped the gun and drew his knife. Unable to reach the thing, there was no other alternative…

He grabbed Chuck by his other shoulder and yanked back. The creature, still holding on, came further into the compartment. Sakai plunged the blade through its left eye. The creature roared in agony, releasing its prize, and hopping backwards, arms raising high to protect its face.

"Hit it!" Sakai said. Chuck straightened out, groaning. His entire arm looked as though a saw blade had come down on it. There was no time to tend to it, change seats, or even be sympathetic. More raptors were descending the hill. "Goddamnit kid, floor the pedal!"

Chuck pressed his foot, gunning the carrier up the creek. The engine struck one of the raptors, knocking it down and crushing it under the wheels. He kept the pedal floored and focused on the hillside.

There! He had found the spot where they could move up.

"Hang on," he called to the group in a strained voice. He hooked to the right to get maximum momentum, then cut the wheel hard to the left and gunned the accelerator. The engine roared, the wheels spitting dirt as they carried the vehicle up the slope.

Gravity caused the passengers to lean downward, right toward the open ramp door. The water splashed just out of view. The raptors were closing in and fast.

Chuck kept the tires floored. The vehicle continued its ascent, finally clearing the top of the hill. The tires immediately found better traction, catching Chuck off guard as the vehicle abruptly tripled its speed. It shot forward for several hundred feet. He yanked the wheel left to avoid a tree, which took him toward another tree. He turned right again, this time realizing they were coming up on the remains of an old fallen tree.

The vehicle bounced up as it came up over the branches. He hit the brakes, took a breath. He was feeling lightheaded now. The left side of the seat was red with his blood. The fallen tree was thick and rotting. There would be no passing over it, even in this vehicle.

Gritting his teeth, he put the carrier in reverse. The carrier shuddered but didn't go anywhere. He looked through the window. The tires were caught on some branches.

"Alright, kid, get in the back," Sakai said. They both disembarked and moved to the rear. "Cutler! Get some dressings on him now!" Kim screamed as she saw Chuck approaching with his arm bloodied.

"Mother of Mary," Cutler mumbled under his breath. He opened his pack and pulled out as much gauze as he could find. Martin and Janet rushed in to assist.

"Jesus, he's torn up," Janet said. She took off her overshirt to use as a sling while Martin tore what was left of the sleeve. He did his best to hide any visceral facial reaction when seeing the damage. The flesh had been minced, dripping large sheets of blood.

"Will he be alright?" Kim asked.

"I'll be fine," Chuck said, forcing a smile.

"Not if we don't stop the bleeding," Cutler said. They tied a strap over his shoulder to cut circulation then packed dressings over the wound. Chuck let out a scream, his nerves shooting through his body like electricity.

"Ward, Landon, help me move the logs. Bordales, you're our new driver. Be ready to gun it."

The marines hustled out of the vehicle. Bordales got in the seat and waited while the marines tried pulling the dead branches out from under it.

"Shit, they won't budge, Sarge," Landon said.

"Alright, let's try pushing. Bordales, back it up when I say—" The three marines lined up along the engine and propped their palms on the front. "NOW! PUSH!"

Muscles strained and tires spun. The carrier backed ever so slowly, scraping dead wood for what felt like eternity. Finally, they heard the crack of a branch, and whatever had jammed the carrier in had come loose. Morgan hit the brakes. Sakai hurried into the passenger seat while Landon and Ward went around the back and onto the loading ramp. Ward took a seat. Landon dropped to his knee and ran his hand along the lower wall near the opening.

"What the hell are you doing?" Ward said.

"Hang on," Landon said. "I'm familiar with these things. There should be a manual lever to get this thing...ah-ha!" He found the panel door and opened it, revealing the lever. He cranked it, gradually lifting the ramp. As he did, Morgan backed the carrier further from its trap. Without the ramp door scraping against the ground, the vehicle was able to move more smoothly.

He only had a couple more feet to go. The vehicle stopped momentarily as Morgan switched gears. Something heavy struck the ceiling. Landon heard the scraping sound of claws on metal. Before he could move, the raptor jutted its head through the open space. It let out an earsplitting shriek, effectively designed to stun its enemies momentarily. Landon's ears rang, his muscles tensing against his will. Talons seized his armor and hauled him up through the opening as easily as if he weighed nothing.

"No!" Ward shouted.

The vehicle moved forward, its driver unaware of the abduction. Morgan heard the screams from the back, then looked in one of the mirrors. She saw the raptor darting into the forest, dragging a struggling Landon in its jaws. She gasped and hit the brakes, then went for her rifle. Sakai grabbed her wrist, stopping her.

"You can't help him," he said. He redirected her eyes to the mirror. Two other raptors ran into view and converged on their fellow marine. Already, his armor had been ripped off. Sickle claws sliced across his abdomen. One of the reptilians had his left arm in its mouth. It twisted and pulled, breaking it off at the elbow. Others bit into his midsection, tearing chunks of flesh free.

Morgan grimaced, then forced herself to floor the accelerator. The carrier raced northwest, as other raptors emerged from the creek. They converged on the fallen prize, eager to get a mouthful of flesh. The fresh blood warmed their insides. It would not last them long. With a burning metabolism, the raptors would soon need more sustenance—and nothing tasted better than human flesh.

CHAPTER 15

"Slow it down," Sakai said. For the past several miles, he had been watching their surroundings carefully. It seemed the raptors had given up the chase for now. They would have to slow anyway, as Morgan had sideswiped at least a dozen trees. The forest had not undergone any development for vehicle passage, thus there was no set trail to their destination. Driving through this forest was like dodging asteroids in space. And the carrier was a big vehicle, not meant for fast maneuvers.

In the back, Cutler continued to pack Chuck's wound. The twenty-four-year-old yelled out with each touch. Cutler had caught glimpses of white during his assessment of the wound. Those teeth had cut through everything. It would take numerous surgeries to fix this arm, and those surgeries would have to commence immediately. But they had no med-pod to halt any infections. There was one up in the Cruiser, but with their dropship destroyed, there was no way of getting up to it.

Chuck yelled again as the medic injected an antibiotic just above the injury.

"Sorry bud," he said, "but this'll help keep any infection from spreading. It should hopefully buy us some time." Kim knelt down beside Chuck and took his other hand.

"Hang in there. We'll get you fixed up shortly," she said. She looked at Cutler with hopeful eyes. The medic forced a nod, though his facial expression betrayed his feelings. "What? He'll make it." Kim spoke definitively, dictating that Chuck would live...and be in one piece. He had to. They had literally just discovered their feelings for one another. It couldn't begin like this.

"How is he?" Janet asked.

Cutler stood up. "We've stopped the bleeding for now. We need to get him to the ship. If we freeze him, we can stop any infection in its tracks and maybe save the arm. Maybe."

"Didn't you just inject something to stop the infection from spreading?"

"Any existing infection, but we're talking about a huge open wound in the middle of a recently discovered planet, home to all kinds of organisms. Until we destroy any contact with the outside world, a new infection will creep its way in within the next twenty-four hours."

"Nice bedside manner," Vance said. She was seated near the front, arms wrapped around her sides. She still felt like she was being crushed. The pain was evident in her voice.

"I've got to say it as it is," Cutler said. "We've got no medical facility out here. We're practically in the early twentieth century. We might have to take that arm off right now."

"Hell no," Chuck muttered.

"Hey kid, I know it hurts, but it's true. I guarantee there's bacteria in the saliva of those things. We don't know enough about it to develop an antibiotic. All I can do is give you what I have and hope it works. That, and maybe amputate your arm if there's no other choice."

"Would he even survive the operation?" Martin asked. Cutler held back from answering. Considering the amount of blood and trauma Chuck had already sustained, and the crude methods Cutler would have to resort to in order to conduct the operation, the likeliness of survival was low. The most important thing right now was to keep him rested and calm. The only way to do that would be to bend the truth. That's where he would have to practice that pesky bedside manner.

"Probably, but we'll hold off for now," he said. He proceeded to tend to Vance's injuries, starting with the shoulder. There wasn't much he could do for her ribcage other than to wrap it tight. The laceration on her shoulder needed immediate attention. Her pale skin had turned completely red. The claws had sunk over an inch deep. It was only through pure luck and timing that it wasn't any worse. He found some more gauze and tape from his pack, soaked it in antibiotics, then applied them to the injuries.

On the front wall was an open panel which led into the driver's seat. Sakai peered through it at his team.

"How's everyone holding up?" he asked.

"Well, aside from the four of us who are dead, I'd say we're going strong," Cutler remarked. He immediately regretted his words. He braced himself mentally for the verbal backlash. Surprisingly, there was none.

"Vance, how you holding up?"

"Never been better, Sarge," she coughed. Cutler stood up to the panel and leaned in, not wanting to be overheard by the others.

"Sarge, we're gonna have to get them to the ship," he said. "That kid's gonna lose that arm if we don't. If I try to remove it, he'll probably bleed out. And don't get me started on bacteria and infections. He needs a proper surgery followed by time in a wash-tank. Vance could use one too to clear out any foreign bacteria."

The Staff Sergeant nodded, then spoke to the whole group, "We're coming up on the dig site. We're gonna stop there, establish a foothold, and make plans from there."

"Are we sure we still want to go that way?" Ward said. His eyes were fixed on the loading ramp, where Landon had been taken right in front of him.

"Yes," Sakai said. "Everyone re-load and prep for dust-off. Vance, you'll stay in here."

"I can fight, Sarge," she said.

"I know you can, that's why I want you to defend this vehicle while we secure the camp and dig site. You civilians, hang on to those weapons we gave you."

"Yes, sir," Martin said. "You think there'll be any pirates there?"

"Something tells me there won't be," Sakai said. *Too bad—I'd rather deal with them than those raptors.*

CHAPTER 16

Mt. Dragoon was a large lump of rock overlooking a large gorge on its northwest side. Upon its discovery, Janet Saldivar thought it to be a dormant volcano, until rock samples collected at the site contained particles of uranium ore. For her, the sight of this mountain was a dreadful one. She had looked forward to seeing the construction equipment all over the place, but doing work for the United World Order, not this band of merciless pirates.

She waited with her fellow surveyors in the carrier, while the marines secured the campsite. It came as no surprise that there was no gunfire. They had passed a couple of Jeeps along the way, their windshields smashed and covered with blood. She could tell it had aged nearly a day. At that point she knew the crew was dead and gone, their flesh stripped to the bone, never to be given a proper funeral or final goodbye. The guilt was overwhelming. She had taken part in the initial survey of the planet and had found no traces of these monsters. Was Ward right? Did she simply miss them? It was possible, those scans were never fully accurate. They were there to help gauge a possible level of threat from the wildlife, but even in this day and age of technology, such assessments could only be done through careful study and observation. It was certainly the case for Malek.

She and Martin stood a few feet back from the boarding ramp, their rifles pointed out at the jungle. They had finally grown used to the feel of the weapon, though they had yet to actually fire them. However, there was no sense of invincibility. Vance's presence was enough to ensure them of that. She was seated behind where Martin stood, her rifle propped on the arm of her seat. The painkiller Cutler had administered took its sweet time to kick in. It made breathing easier, but it still hurt when she stood, especially with the rifle in hand.

Kim was kneeled on the aisle next to Chuck, who was laying on his back as comfortably as possible. She had her pistol in hand, though she wasn't watching the outside. Instead, she was watching Chuck, who in turn, was watching her.

"Maybe they'll get me one of those bionic arms," he joked. Kim forced a smile. She knew it was his way of accepting the realities of his situation.

"I'll hand it to you kid. I'm impressed you were able to drive this thing after what that raptor did to you," Martin said.

"Well…" Chuck looked away. "Can't say I did it well. I drove us right into that brush and got the marine with the mustache killed."

"Ah-ah, no," Vance said. "The only people to be blame are Gillion and his damned pirates. And they got what they deserved. You did well, Chuck Campbell. You got us out of a tight spot. And we will do right by you. We'll get you up to our cruiser and put you on ice. When you wake up, you'll be feeling a lot better."

"Thanks, Marine," Chuck said.

Vance's commlink crackled before Sakai's voice came through. *"Sakai to Vance, area is secured. Have Martin drive you up the ridge for three hundred yards".*

"Ten-four, Sarge." Vance glanced at Martin. "You heard him, Dr. Fry."

"You got it," he said. He stepped out the back and went around to the driver's seat, then accelerated between a patch of trees.

****

It only took a few moments to enter the vast clearing. Up ahead was the enormous rock structure that was Mount Dragoon. Up close, it looked like a never-ending hill going up at a fairly consistent forty-five-degree angle. Huge rocks extended from its rigid surface like blisters.

Martin took the vehicle up as far as he could, coming to the ridge that Sakai had described. It led to a large, relatively flat shelf of rock where the pirates had initially made camp. From a bird's perspective, it looked like an alcove that had been carved into the side of the mountain. In a way, it was. She saw the digger parked several meters to the left-hand side. It had a large hydraulic arm, much like a backhoe. Instead of a scoop, however, it contained a huge drill on its end. There were tread marks along the ground where bulldozers had scooped away the excess sediment.

The marines were standing by, waiting for the rest of the group to arrive. As Martin parked, Ward, Morgan, and Cutler hurried along to the back to help Chuck and Vance out. There were a few sunblock tarps standing to provide shade, though they weren't especially needed at the moment. The sunlight was gradually fading as it sank into the horizon.

Martin stepped out first and gazed at what remained of the settlement. There were tents, tables, a dry campfire, all overturned and smashed. Bloodstains were smeared everywhere, now dry and flaking. Weapons and cartridges littered the ground amidst the ruins. As the group predicted, the raptors swept through the camp like an evil flood, taking any life in its wake.

At the back of the alcove was a small cave which led nearly twenty feet into the mountain. The marks left by the digger that created it were still visible. There was black residue on the ground from the enormous drill-bits, and much of the loose rock hadn't been shoveled out.

"Is that where you found the uranium?" Vance asked.

"No," Janet answered. She pointed to a path that led beyond the camp. It went around the mountainside, just wide enough for the construction vehicles to pass over. "Did you find anyone alive over there?" Janet asked Sakai. It was a redundant question. Sakai answered anyway.

"No, I'm sorry. But we did find something you might find interesting." Janet's interest piqued, and she and Martin followed the Staff Sergeant along the path while the others stood watch.

They walked for several hundred feet, leaning hard to the left as the path led them to a steep side of the mountain. Tread tracks were visible in the sediment from the heavy construction vehicles and cargo trucks.

"I see the cranes," Martin said. "The ridge is up straight ahead." After a few more minutes of walking, they came to the edge of the Dragoon Ridge, overlooking an enormous gorge. The bottom was nearly five hundred feet down. Brown soil had originally covered the uranium deposit. The cranes had to dig over fifty feet in order to find the ore.

The mountainside had a few scattered trees. Though spaced out, they were as large as those that grew in the dense forest, the leaves not having to compete for sunlight. Beneath one of them were the cargo trucks, each carrying one of the uranium storage containers. They were sealed tight, securing thousands of pounds of ore and blocking the radiation from the outside world.

"At least the uranium didn't fall into the wrong hands," Martin said. "Had those pirates gotten it off the planet, they would've sold it to any one of the hundreds of terrorist sponsors in the galaxy." He turned to Sakai. "Was this what you wanted to show us?"

"No. This is." Sakai led them further down the ridge to a pile of discarded sediment. It was from the soil that had covered the uranium. Janet's jaw dropped as she saw the hollow eggshells. There were dozens of them, their insides slightly moist from the yoke residue that kept their occupants alive.

"Holy shit," she said. The eggs were the size of footballs. The outer shell looked almost like rock. She got closer and knelt down for a closer view. It almost appeared as though the eggs had fused with the rocks. "It is...are they...fossilized?"

"Doc, you're the geologist, not me," Sakai said.

"Sorry, I was thinking out loud," Janet said. She never looked away from the fascinating find. She tried counting the number of specimens but there were too many fragments to know exactly how many there were.

"Dr. Saldivar, be careful," Martin said. "This soil came from the uranium deposit. It might be radioactive."

"I want to examine them," Janet said.

"I understand that, but we need to focus on getting out of here," Martin said. He put his hands on her shoulder, gently, and pulled her away.

"Not anywhere tonight," Sakai said. Martin looked at him, defensively. "Sorry, Docs, but look there." He pointed at the horizon. "We're losing light fast."

"You want to set up camp? With those things out there?" Martin said.

"Do I want to? Hell no," Sakai said. "But you saw how it is to drive in that forest in the daytime. How do you think it'll be at night with those things out there?"

"What about Chuck?" Martin asked. "He needs to get to your ship."

"We've come this far. We could go the rest of the way to the shuttle camp," Janet said.

"You know where it is?" Sakai said.

"Five miles north of here, roughly," Janet said.

"Yeah, Doc?" Sakai said. "I seem to remember you saying something about some marshes, home to some giant species." Janet swallowed. Her concern had caused her to completely forget about it. "You said it yourself, Doctor, it's hard enough traveling between those swamps in the day. How do you think it'll be at night?"

"I'm sorry, Sergeant," Janet admitted. "You're right. We can't go wandering about in the dark. We'll be slaughtered. We'll be better off setting up camp for the night. We'll make a go for it in the morning."

"We can't wait. Chuck needs medical attention," Martin persisted.

Sakai's patience wore thin. He squared up with the physicist, his tone hard enough to grind rock. "You think I'm unaware? You think I don't have a marine who's injured over there? What about the four who are dead?" Martin took a step back and absorbed the facts.

"I—I'm sorry," he said. There was nothing else said. Sakai inhaled deeply through his nose, calming himself. There was no malintent behind the doctor's concerns. Like a rational, decent human being, he just wanted to get his people to safety.

"Don't worry about it," Sakai said. He gave Martin a gentle tap on the arm, then looked back at Morgan. "Bordales, have the squad set up perimeter defenses. Set up flares, claymores, and tripwires. Set up as many as you can near the tree line in case those bastards try to sneak in at night. Also, line the ledge with electro-wire, in case any of those bastards somehow get past the trees. It'll give them a nice surprise if they try and climb up. That said, this area is a fairly open space, so it won't be as easy for those pricks to sneak up on us."

"Yes, sir," Morgan said.

Janet knelt again by the assortment of eggshells. "Well, if we're gonna stay the night, then I want to examine these samples. It looks like some of the equipment is still intact. I have a theory about how these creatures appeared all of a sudden."

"There's protective gear we can wear at camp," Martin said.

"Good. Let's get those on and get these collected before the sun goes down," Janet said.

"Will it be safe? Isn't it radioactive?" Sakai asked.

"Uranium tends to be more harmful from chemical effects rather than radiation," Martin said. "Uranium isotopes emit alpha particles with little penetrating ability. We can keep these samples in the cave, everyone else will be safe, as long as they don't touch it with their bare hands."

"Fine. Let's hurry it up then," Sakai said.

CHAPTER 17

Morgan shivered, the night air clinging to her as she walked along the ledge. When the sun went down, so did the temperature by twenty-five degrees. While still warm, it felt chilly by comparison. She kept her rifle pointed out into the rocky slope below. She could barely see the tree line a few hundred feet out. It wasn't until nightfall when she realized that Malek had two moons. They were like silver bulbs in the sky, casting the sun's reflection over the vast forest.

The only lights came from inside the cave, where Martin and Janet were busy analyzing the samples taken from the dig. Kim and Chuck were laying together just outside of it, embracing the cool air. Vance was on a sleeping bag, though sleep would be a near impossible task. There was no comfortable position for her to lay in thanks to her injuries. Her discomfort was displayed in an unmoving grimace. On the other hand, Ward was out cold.

Cutler gave Chuck another dose of painkiller. He groaned as the needle entered his arm, right above the sensitive area. The sling that Janet had made him kept it tucked nice and close. He saw Morgan impatiently walking along the ledge.

"Hey," he said. "They're not gonna get past our flammables. Why don't you have some rations."

"Not hungry," Morgan replied.

"I hate to do the cliched speech about eating to stay strong," Cutler said. He grabbed an MRE and walked over to her. "But, it's true. As a member of this group, you have a duty to keep yourself in a good fighting condition. Don't want you being worn down because you didn't sustain your body." He extended the box to her. "You sit. I'll stand guard. Doctor's orders."

Morgan snickered. "Thanks." She took the MRE and walked toward the back of the camp. She sat on a flattened out rock near Kim and Chuck. The latter was wrapped tight in a sleeping bag. She could tell the young man was in considerable discomfort, which made sleeping very difficult.

They were in the middle of some conversation about the digger.

"I'm just saying we could put it to use tomorrow," Kim said. "Someone could operate it and drive ahead of the carrier. The driller has a back loader. We could use it to lift debris out of the way."

"Those things are pains in the asses to operate. I'd do it if I had both hands," Chuck said.

"I could do it," Kim said.

"You might have a feel for it after handling the loader back at the shuttle," Chuck said, "but it's a slow vehicle. It'd probably cause more trouble than it's worth."

"If you say so," Kim said, conceding defeat with a sigh. She watched Morgan take her helmet off. Stray strands of hair fell loose and swayed over her face. She untied her hair, then retied it to get it right.

"I love that color," Kim said. Morgan forced a smile. She didn't think the dye would stand out in the dark.

"Thanks. I do too," she said.

"I thought they didn't allow that in the Marines," Kim said.

"They typically don't. Let's just say I was able to get around that regulation," Morgan said. Not wanting to press the subject, she glanced down at Chuck. "How are you feeling?"

"God, this hurts like a bitch," he muttered.

"Fuck this planet," Kim replied. "Don't know about you guys, but I'm ready to go home."

"Where are you from?" Morgan asked.

"Zar-Five," Kim said.

"The ring stations?!" Morgan said. She worried she sounded disrespectful. "Sorry, I just couldn't stand living around all that steel. No fresh air or real outdoor experience." Her mind flashed to her time in prison, then to the years spent on the ship during cargo deliveries.

"No, don't be sorry. Because you're right," Kim said. "They have gardens and wild-park areas, but you can tell the plants are artificial. That's one of the things that attracted me to this career. I wanted to see a planet like this—of course, I wasn't anticipating dinosaurs coming to life and chasing me."

"Take it from me, it kind of sours the experience," Chuck groaned.

"What about you, Marine," Kim said, "where are you from?"

"Earth. Florida, to be more precise," Morgan replied.

"You got family waiting for you there?" Kim asked. Morgan thought for a moment, unsure if she wanted to answer the question honestly.

"A son," Morgan said. She was surprised that she admitted it.

"Really? How old?" Kim asked.

"Six," Morgan said. She opened her MRE and began eating the rations, hoping the topic would change on its own. She thought more about Jamie, which only served to depress herself. Every time she envisioned him, it was based on memories from her last contact with him, when he had just turned three. He still had those adorable chubby baby cheeks, and his speech was just starting to come along. Now he was six. He probably looked entirely different now, so much so that she wondered if she'd even recognize him if she passed him in the street.

"I have one the same age," Kim said. Morgan looked up. Her bewilderment was plain on her face. Kim was in her early-twenties at best. If she had a child that was six, then that meant— "Yeah," Kim said, answering the unspoken question, "Bad decisions when I was seventeen. But I'm not sorry. I'm just glad they wouldn't allow him on this trip with me, considering…you know."

"What's he like?" Morgan asked.

"Like any six-year-old," Kim said. "Got a heart of gold. Loves puzzles. I try and keep him away from the electronics. Then again, everything designed for kids these days is electronic. Even the books. I took this job because it was the first decent one I could get after graduating, though I'm having second thoughts. I didn't really consider all the time apart."

"Take it from me," Morgan said, "don't take this time for granted. Be with your boy as much as you can. This is a precious time."

"Thanks for saying that," Kim said. She sighed. "He and I have been writing every day, until our ship was hijacked. Each time I read his messages, I wish I was there with him. You probably know how that is." Kim noticed Morgan's expression sadden. "Does he not write you?"

"No," Morgan said. "I write him all the time but he doesn't write back. It's…complicated."

"You know, it's funny: kids drive you insane and make you wish for a break. But the moment you get that break, all you can think about is the little rascal."

"I understand that," Morgan said.

"And they think about their parents more than we might think," Kim said.

"Yours might. I don't know about mine," Morgan said.

"Oh, don't be such a bummer," Kim said. "I bet, when we get up to your cruiser, you'll find an inbound message on your computer. In fact, I'll bet you a hundred Smith-Dollars." Morgan laughed. "I'm serious. One hundred Smiths that you'll find a message from your son."

"I sure could use the money. Clearly, you're eager to lose it."

"We'll just have to see." Kim and Morgan shook hands and shared a chuckle.

A red flash engulfed the campsite, causing everyone to jump to their feet. Sakai tore out of the cave, rifle in hand. The flare had shot from the tree line, its flickering red light illuminating the whole mountainside.

There was a deep roar and the sound of pounding feet.

"Everyone get into position!" Sakai said. "Watch those corners. Stay sharp! Ward, shine a light down there on the double!"

The marine's mind was still hazy as he looked around for the camp's spotlight. He found it and turned it on. A white beam of light lit the sky. He rotated it and aimed it downward toward the sound of footsteps. He saw the crest and the horn, and his nerves settled when he realized what it was.

"You damned...burrito-saurus, whatever the hell you're called!" he said. The dinosaur walked in a tight circle, still puzzled from the sudden burst of fire that spat from the ground.

"Styracosaurus," Janet corrected him. Ward glanced back at her. She was still wearing the protective gear for examining the eggshells.

"Whatever." The styracosaurus grunted, then sniffed around. As large as a tank, it moved with grace. It had calmed itself, realizing there was no threat. It followed the white light and saw the strange herd of creatures it had encountered earlier. Ward kept the light on it.

"Look at that," he said. The light revealed a few gashes in the creature's shoulder. "I was wondering how he avoided those raptors...turns out he didn't."

"He's lucky," Janet said. "A pack of raptors are designed for taking on large prey."

"See his horn?" Ward said. He tilted the light slightly downward, putting it in the herbivore's face. The tip of its horn was dark red. "Looks like one of those bastards won't be bothering anyone anymore. I hope it was paaaaiiinful." The dinosaur grunted in protest and turned away. "Oh, fine. If you don't like the light, I won't shine it on ya anymore."

"Arguing even on your first date. Pretty typical for you, Ward," Cutler said.

"She's about the size of woman he goes after," Morgan remarked. The group shared a laugh.

"Who says it's a woman?" Kim added. The laughter intensified. Ward glanced at her.

"You too, huh? Thanks."

The marines stepped back from the ledge. Vance coughed then hunched over. She had instinctively jumped to her feet, ready to meet the call to arms. Unfortunately, she wasn't used to doing it with broken ribs. Morgan took her by the arm and helped her back to her sleeping bag. Vance sat up and leaned against a rock.

"Bordales, take it from me...don't let a dinosaur fall on you." Her chuckle turned into another pained cough.

"I'll do my best," Morgan replied.

"I'll resume watch," Cutler said.

"Three hours. After that, Ward will take a turn. Everyone else, try and get some rest. We leave at sunrise," Sakai said. He followed Martin and Janet back into the cave.

They had several egg samples stored on a table. Luckily the pirates had kept Janet's tools and microscopes in fair condition. She had scraped some rock samples from the eggshells and ran it through the radiometric machine, along with several samples from other rock near the ore.

"So, this machine helps determine how old the rocks are?" Sakai said.

"Yes," Janet said.

"As simple as that?" Sakai said.

"Yes," Janet repeated. "The hardest part was separating the samples from the shells."

"Why do you need them separated?" Sakai asked.

"Because, if the shells aren't the same age as the rock, then it might interfere with the reading," Janet said. "You want me to give you a lesson on geology and radiometric dating, or do you want me to finish this up?"

Sakai stepped back, giving the scientists their space. He didn't understand any of this stuff, nor did he really care to. He stood back and watched the machine light up. Red interior lights flashed as it scanned the samples. The process seemed to last forever. During this time, Janet continued looking over the egg fragments. He noticed that she was putting them into different piles. One pile contained eggs that were the size of footballs. Another large pile had eggs that were somewhat smaller. Aside from those were two larger eggs that were clearly not connected to either species. It was the best Janet could do with her limited data and tools to segregate the species.

Finally, the machine finished its scan. A large screen flashed on the side, reading the results.

"Forty-five million years old," she said.

"My God," Martin said. "I can't believe it."

"With no existing records to compare these samples with, I can't confirm with a hundred percent certainty which species these belong to. However, I think I can apply the process of elimination based on what we've observed so far," she said. She pointed at the largest group of eggs. "These ones are the raptors." She moved to another pile of smaller eggs. "These ones are the pterodactyls. And these other two, well, one's the styracosaurus. The other is something else."

"True living fossils," Martin said in awe.

"Wait, hang on…" Sakai said. He stumbled over his words until he managed to articulate his question without sounding like a buffoon. "Are you suggesting these raptors are supposed to be extinct on this planet like on Earth?"

"There's theories of planets sharing similar ecosystems as well as similar evolutionary developments," Janet said. "I think Malek had a dinosaur age that ultimately went extinct. That's why we didn't see any during the initial survey of the planet's surface."

"And that these eggs somehow survived all these years until the pirates forced your crew to dig them up?"

"That's the theory," Janet said. "They probably tossed the eggs aside with the rest of the useless sediment. Hell, they probably didn't even know they were eggs. From the outside, they look just like rocks."

"There's all kinds of ore down in that gorge that's completely new to us," Martin said. "The ore must've preserved the eggs during all of these centuries. When they were dug up, the creatures hatched. The radioactivity caused them to grow rapidly. They hatched, fed on small animals while they grew. Once they got big, they decided to hunt bigger prey: humans."

"This doesn't make sense," Sakai said. "These eggs were all in the same spot? The pterodactyls? The Styracosaurus? Whatever else that might be running around out there? These eggs were all in the same spot? I'm no scientist, but I don't think animals, especially hostile ones, tend to share nesting sites."

"No, they don't," Janet said, "but I have a theory. Slightly far-fetched, but then again…what isn't far-fetched at this point?"

"I'm all ears," Sakai said.

"There are several species across the animal kingdom that feed on the eggs of others," she began. "It is my belief, that millions of years ago, the pack of raptors that birthed these eggs had sent out hunters to bring down large prey. During their hunts, they would find eggs from other nests to feed to their young. That's why we have so many species in a similar location. These other species were brought to the nest to be eaten. Then, something happened. There was a cataclysm of some sort, much like the asteroid collision that killed the dinosaurs of Earth. Sensing something was wrong, the raptors buried their eggs under the uranium ore for protection. Because of the ravine, or some divine circumstance, the eggs survived and were preserved by the ore. For forty-five million years. Until finally, Gillion and his pirates dug them up. Maybe it was the contact with the air that caused them to hatch. Maybe a temperature change. Either way, these things are alive now."

Sakai stood silent, his mind pondering the doctor's theory. Had he not already seen the lizards, he likely would have broken into laughter. Instead, he felt a headache coming on. This all seemed so impossible. Yet, somehow, it was real.

"I need a drink," he said.

Janet started to remove the protective gear. "Me too. Too bad the damn pirates took our brandy."

"What a shame," Sakai said. He stepped outside and gazed once more at the tree line. Those raptors were lurking somewhere out there. "How many do you think there are?"

"No way of telling," Janet said. "I guarantee these eggs are only a fraction of the overall pack."

"That's what I was afraid of. Well, let's just hope they don't decide to hunt over this way. In the meantime, let's get some sleep. The sun will be up in six hours."

It wasn't a suggestion. The scientists removed their gear and used them as tarps to cover the samples. They each found a sleeping bag and picked a spot to sleep.

Sakai stepped outside. Most of the group was already out, including Chuck and Kim. He found a spot on the far right and sat up against a boulder. He stared out into the forest, his rifle in his lap. It took several minutes, until finally, he zoned out.

****

In the hours that followed, he fell into a world of strange images that would make no sense to the conscious mind. But to the unconscious, everything had meaning. One dream led to the next. In one occasion, he was back in basic training, crawling through mud. In the next, he was in the woods, watching trucks tearing through the wilderness. He tasted dirt. He could see the construction worker crawling into the machine. The engine started with a triumphant roar.

It roared again. He could feel the earth shake as the mighty tree-logger moved. On its front were enormous buzz-saws that sliced through the trees. But he couldn't hear any cutting. Instead, he heard crunching and smashing. A tree fell, but it was somewhere far in the distance. The engine roared again, like that of some gargantuan beast.

He then saw red lights blinding him. They took to the sky like astro-propelled rockets. It was like fire in the sky. Shouting followed, along with the sound of footsteps.

****

Sakai's eyes shot open. The red lights were not a figment of his imagination; they were as real as the rock he sat on. Reality struck and he sprang to his feet.

"Talk to me, Marines! What do you see?"

Ward was on one knee, scanning the area with his binoculars.

"Something big. Probably that horned-dinosaur again," he said. "Whatever it is, it went back into the trees."

"I'd prefer confirmation, not speculation," Sakai said. "You civilians get back into the cave."

"There's movement," Ward announced. Its thunderous footsteps shook the ground. Branches crackled, birds soared high for dear life. A claymore detonated, triggering a deep roar. Now the footsteps were faster. Flares blasted high into the sky. The smashing of branches intensified, as though the enormous beast within was at war with the forest.

The team heard the sound of impact, followed by the booming crack of a tree trunk snapping in half. Succeeding that crack was a wooden squeal, so loud and lively it appeared the tree was crying out in pain as it teetered outward. It initially fell slowly as it cleared the branches of neighboring trees, then smashed hard into the ground, triggering one of the other claymores the team had set up.

Through the newly formed gap in the forest, the monstrosity stomped out into the open slope on powerful hind legs.

"Jesus," Janet said. The beast was a theropod, a biped reptile that, when it stood with a straight posture, would tower over thirty feet high. Three-fingered arms were coiled under its chest like a praying mantis. Eighteen-inch fangs jutted from its upper jaw. Three-toed feet created small craters wherever it stepped. Behind it, an enormous whip-like tail, with a length matching its body, thrashed the trees behind it.

"Guys…" Morgan muttered.

"Fucking T-Rex…" Ward said.

"Ceratosaurus," Janet said. The creature lowered its posture and stuck its head into the white beam of light. On its nose was a curved horn, appearing like a shark's fin. It turned its head and saw the bite-sized creatures standing on the rock ledge several hundred feet ahead. It stood straight, its head rising high above the height of the ledge. It let out an ear-splitting roar, leaned forward, and charged the camp.

CHAPTER 18

"Withdraw! Everyone in the cave!" Sakai's voice was barely heard over the bursts of gunfire. Each rifle round sparked like a firecracker after striking the Ceratosaurus' thick, pebbly skin.

Morgan and Janet lifted Vance to her feet and pulled her into the cave. Ward and Cutler continued firing at the beast, while Kim and Martin struggled to get Chuck up. Dust and gravel rained from the roof of the cave as they hurried inside.

The enormous beast was now at the ledge. It snapped its jaws at Ward. He yelled as those jaws clamped shut inches from his chest. More bullets exploded along the creature's snout.

"Get your asses in here!" Sakai shouted from the cave entrance. He continued laying cover fire as his marines closed the distance. The creature roared angrily. The bullets, though unable to break its granite-like skin, still stung as though the creature was being assaulted by an invisible horde of wasps. It reared up and lifted one of its feet over the ledge. With a single bound, it was on level ground with the group. It leaned forward and charged the cave.

Sakai turned and dove. "Get back!"

Chunks of rock exploded inward. The Ceratosaurus raked its horn along the edges, sawing away at the entrance. Already, the entrance had doubled in size, allowing the beast to jut its incredibly large head into the small tunnel. Screams and gunfire filled the confined space. Ears rang and visions blurred.

Sakai was on his back, buried under a layer of pebbles and dust. He felt the creature's breath come over him like a hot wind. He looked down and saw the jaws opening wide, baring down on him. Instinct took over. He rolled to the left. He felt a tremor of impact sweep the cave floor. The creature's snout missed, scooping up nothing but stale tasting dust. It spat and roared. Saliva and hot air blasted the tunnel like dragon fire. The intense vibration shook the interior, causing debris to rain down from the ceiling. Huge rocks as large and heavy as bowling balls rained free, smashing into the floor.

Sakai saw a shift above. There was a chunk of rock directly above his face, rocking back and forth. With a large crack, it came free. He rolled again, this time right back toward those jaws he was so desperately trying to avoid. The rock smashed like a ceramic pot. He kicked his feet to scoot himself away from the Ceratosaurus' mouth. Its eye rolled down and locked onto him.

It tried to snap, but was just out of reach. Frustrated, it writhed its whole body. It was now lying on its stomach, trying to slither into the cave like a snake. Its two arms were protruding in through the mouth of the cave, clawing the floor.

Most of the overhead lights had gone out, save for one near the back. Its flickering light glistened over the ten humans, who were jampacked at the end of the cave.

More gunshots rang out. The bullets struck along its snout, causing the dinosaur to roar again. As its mouth opened, one of the bullets found its way into the soft flesh inside. The sudden pain caused an instinctive jolt backwards. Its head struck the roof of the cave, causing another onslaught of rocks.

"Drive it back!" Cutler said. He couldn't even hear himself speak over the deafening gunfire. The confined noise made his head feel warped. That combined with the surging adrenaline caused dizziness and confusion. Despite this, he kept gunning at the beast, hoping for a lucky shot. With his senses warped, he was completely unaware of the rock shifting above him, nor did he hear the crack of its detachment from the cave ceiling.

Cutler felt a heavy impact smash over the back of his helmet like a sledgehammer, knocking him forward. The creature saw the little critter with the strange defense mechanism stagger into range. It hyperextended its jaws and tilted its neck until its head was almost horizontal. The jaws closed like a vice, instantly snapping arms, ribs. Cutler tried screaming but couldn't, as those enormous teeth had punctured his lungs.

The creature wiggled its body and pushed with its claws, freeing itself from the self-imposed entrapment. Like a dog with a chew toy, it shook its prey violently. It tasted the fresh blood of its victim, spurring it on to mash it up further. It backed away and proceeded to chomp. Cutler let out one final groan before those teeth mashed him into pulp. Legs and arms fell free, his trunk grinded up and swallowed.

Not to let anything go to waste, it found the limbs and scooped them into its mouth with its tongue. It licked its chops then redirected its gaze at the cave. It didn't want to abandon its prey, but had no desire to risk getting stuck. It would resort to the tactic its ancestors would use to frighten prey out of their burrows: it would dig them out.

It rammed the rock wall, splintering the edges with its horn. It pivoted on its feet and lashed its tail, then raked the edges with its huge talons.

The entire cave was now entirely filled with dust. Nobody had a line of sight greater than a few feet. They felt the aftershock of the dinosaur's impacts and the sound of rock falling away.

"It's widening the cave," Janet said.

"Yeah, no shit," Ward said. "In a few minutes, it's gonna have free access to this buffet. And we've got nowhere to go. Sarge! We've got to run for it!"

"I'm well aware," Sakai said, spitting grey dust from his mouth. He chambered a grenade with the lever-action on his under-barrel launcher. "Everyone, get ready to move. If this doesn't kill it, it's gotta be enough to drive it away at least."

As he spoke, the beast struck again. The whole interior vibrated. There were crumbling sounds from above. All eyes went to the ceiling and saw that the whole roof was about to come down on them. The group scattered. Rocks as large as car tires showered the cave.

Morgan jumped to the right, barely avoiding a huge chunk of rock.

"Look out!" It was Vance's voice. Morgan felt a jolt from behind as Vance pushed her out of the way. The rock that was breaking free above her came loose, striking Vance in her already injured shoulder. The marine fell, yelling in pain. Morgan hurried to her side and pulled her to the furthest wall. Her shoulder was visibly smashed, practically forming a cavity in her upper torso.

"Damn it, Ruth," Morgan said.

The group continued moving back and forth to avoid the rocks. Martin and Janet moved Chuck out of the way. The Ceratosaurus struck again. They heard crumbling rocks overhead. There was no need to look up, for it was clear there was going to be more debris coming down. Martin pushed Janet and Chuck out of the way, then turned and ran blindly. He heard chunks of mountain smash down behind him.

He bumped into someone, nearly knocking them down. He saw the glasses and dark hair, realizing it to be Kim. They looked to each other, then back at the entrance, realizing they were only a few feet away from it. The creature slammed against it, then backed away.

They looked back, realizing that several boulder-sized rocks had fallen between them and the rest of the group. It would take a little digging for them to get out.

"Damn thing's trying to widen the entrance. It doesn't realize it's burying its meal," Martin said.

"What do we do?" Kim said.

"It's gonna hit again, then back up," Martin said, watching the Ceratosaurus. "When it turns, we'll have to make a break for it."

"But what about—"

"We'll lure it away so they can escape," Martin said. The Ceratosaurus turned at the ledge and prepared to charge. "Get ready. When I say, go for the carrier. Bring it up to the entrance and get everyone inside." He pulled her back a few steps as the Ceratosaurus' mighty feet stomped the ground outside. It threw its whole body over the cave entrance, snapping portions from the edges. It gazed at its work, deciding to widen it a little further before attempting to fish out its prey. It turned around and started for the ledge.

"NOW!" Martin said. He pushed Kim ahead of him. It took her a few steps to muster the courage to run. They were out in the open, completely vulnerable to the beast's wrath. In the span of a second, she had gone from being frozen from fear to running faster than she ever had in her life.

The creature took its position to charge the cave again. Before it charged, it noticed the two little creatures running along the small slope to its left. A deep roar echoed into the sky.

They could hear it running. The ground rippled with each footstep. Kim was a couple yards ahead of him, her youth providing an advantage. He, on the other hand, was middle aged and out of shape.

"Keep going!" Martin shouted. Even as he spoke, he knew they wouldn't make it. At least, not both of them. He accepted his fate, said a brief prayer in his mind, then darted to the left. He still had the gun that the marines had given him. Without even aiming, he pointed it over his shoulder and fired. The recoil nearly shook it from his grasp. However, one of those rounds must've landed because the beast let out an agonized roar.

Kim looked back. She immediately noticed that Martin wasn't right behind her and that the dinosaur had changed direction. That's when she saw Martin off to the side, near the end of the ledge. He fired from the hip, the LED flashing red.

"Go!" he yelled to her.

"NO! DR. FRY!"

"It's okay," the physicist said silently. The Ceratosaurus closed in and slammed its jaws shut over his body. It shook its head back and forth, the jaws mashing his body. It tilted its head back and swallowed him whole. The meat had no sooner entered its gullet when it turned its attention on the other. Kim screamed and continued running.

The carrier was a few hundred feet ahead. The beast was already starting to charge. She wouldn't even make it halfway before it caught up to her. Accepting this, there was only one other option: the digger. It was much closer. The Ceratosaurus would probably smash the cab to bits, but it was better than doing nothing.

She veered a bit to the right and hopped up over the tracks. She dove into the cab and latched the door shut. Not that it would do much good; the dinosaur would make short work of the glass and steel frame. She pressed the starter repeatedly, remembering Chuck's instructions to the crew during their initial approach to Malek.

Please, God, don't let the battery be dead.

To her relief, the engine came alive with a heavy rumble. Spotlights flashed on, bright enough to bring the oncoming monster to a halt. It dug its heels into the earth, then snapped its jaws at the air. This inanimate object had suddenly come alive and was making all kinds of noises it perceived as aggressive.

Behind those 'aggressive' lights and noises was a young woman who was nearly hysterical. The beast was less than twenty feet away, swaying its head left and right, sizing up its opponent. She hyperventilated, watching the monster baring its teeth with a low growl. Its teeth were stained red from Martin's blood.

He had given his life so she could live on. She would not let it be in vain. She looked over the controls, finally finding the one reading *drill rotation*. She pressed the button. The massive drill on the big metal arm began to rotate. The Ceratosaurus stepped back, unsure of what this metal opponent was attempting.

"That's right, back off," Kim said. Of course, it wouldn't do so for long. At best, she had a few seconds before it would make its move. She looked at the controls. Thankfully, they were similar enough to those from the loader that she could figure out what was what. She grabbed the lever and shifted into first gear. The tracks rolled the vehicle forward. She shifted into second gear, then third, racing the driller straight into the beast. She grabbed the arm controls and extended the drill toward the beast's head, then intensified rotation.

The Ceratosaurus backed up, then tilted its head to the left, avoiding the drill. After sidestepping, it snapped its jaws over the arm. Its teeth failed to penetrate the odd 'flesh'. The sudden pain caused it to let go and move back. It cocked its jaws and licked its teeth. It had learned that biting this thing would do no good. It would have to smash it, perhaps break the shell to find any soft flesh inside. Regardless, backing down was not an option.

Kim rotated the driller and coiled the arm back. It was like a scorpion's tail, its 'stinger' pointed directly at the dinosaur. Shifting back into gear, she lashed the arm out. The Ceratosaurus bounced to the right like an insect, then charged the platform. It raised a clawed foot and brought it down on the track, tilting the vehicle slightly. Kim screamed briefly, then swung the arm like a beam, striking the Ceratosaurus and driving it back. The two stared down for a moment, and sized each other up.

Kim sucked in a deep breath, then let out a long exhale, forcing her fears out with it. Her hands tightened over the controls. She thought of her six-year-old. He needed his mommy, and no damn lizard was going to take her away from him.

"Waiting on you," she said to the beast. It roared, scraped the ground with its talons. Then simultaneously, both titans charged each other.

"Come on, everyone," Sakai said. They shuffled the rocks out of the way, finally creating a path to the entrance. They could hear the violent turmoil outside, though they weren't yet sure what was happening.

Sakai took point. Morgan and Ward were right behind him, working together to carry Vance. Behind them were Janet and Chuck. Despite his low energy and blood pressure, the young man pressed forward. The group reached the entrance and saw the driller and Ceratosaurus engaged in mortal combat.

Chuck caught a glimpse of the driver through the cockpit. It was Kim!

"Oh, God! She's gonna get killed!" he said.

"We'll help her, but we need to get you into the carrier first," Sakai said.

"But…"

"Go!" Sakai said. The group ran as fast as they could, while searching for Martin. There was no trace, except for an abandoned rifle near the shallow end of the ledge. Ward took a moment to shine his light over it, seeing the blood that covered the weapon. Martin Fry's fate was clear.

"Oh…Martin…" Janet muttered. She would have to mourn later. She followed the marines to the back of the carrier. Morgan and Ward helped Vance into a seat and strapped her in. She groaned loudly, her shoulder completely unrecognizable. Her arm hung limp, rendering her unable to use a rifle. She drew her sidearm and held it over her lap.

"Ruth, you didn't have to—"

"Shut up, convict," Vance muttered. "It's what we do. Besides, the way I see it, you oughta get back to your kid."

Sakai peeked in from the edge of the ramp. "Hang in there, Vance."

"You betcha, Sarge," she said.

"Bordales, you're back in the driver's seat," Sakai ordered.

"What about Kim?" Chuck said.

"Let us handle that," Sakai said. He and Morgan boarded the front seats and found themselves staring at the battle taking place ahead.

"She's gonna get herself killed," Morgan said.

"I know..." Sakai said. He checked his under-barrel grenade launcher. Unfortunately, with the driller so close, he couldn't risk firing it without risking Kim's safety.

The sun was starting to peek over the horizon. Golden beams stretched over the forest.

Sakai's eyes went to the ledge. A few pebbles fell free to the short distance below. An idea came to mind. If Kim could drive it off the ledge, the fall would hopefully stun the beast enough for her to get away. Maybe. It was only a ten-foot drop, but for something as heavy as the Ceratosaurus, it would hurt more than a mere trip-and-fall.

"Be ready to floor it," he told Morgan. He got out of the carrier and ran ahead until he was forty or fifty feet away from the clash.

The Ceratosaurus lunged. Its short, but muscular arms lashed out for the drill arm, holding tight. Its tail lashed the cockpit, causing glass to burst. Kim screamed, then reversed. The creature's grip loosened but didn't give way. She swung the arm, the edge of the spiraling drill scraping the predator's neck. Flakes of skin were torn away, causing the dinosaur to lurch back in pain.

She noticed something moving to the right. Not something—someone! It was the Staff Sergeant. He was pointing, seemingly at the dinosaur. No...past the dinosaur. It was like having a boxing manager calling out directions from her corner of the ring.

At that moment, he fired his grenade launcher at the beast. The grenade detonated over its hip. The Ceratosaurus roared in pain and staggered to the side. Another grenade struck over its shoulder. It staggered again, barely able to keep from toppling to its side.

Sakai couldn't believe it. Other than a few lacerations and burns, the grenades barely had any effect on the beast. Regardless, it was off balance, providing Kim the opportunity she needed. She put the digger into full throttle and rammed the Ceratosaurus as though driving a bulldozer. It roared and stumbled to the side, its foot coming off the edge of the rock platform.

Kim locked the controls in place, opened the starboard door, then dove to the ground. The driller continued racing behind her at full force, driving the Ceratosaurus over the edge of the cliff. The monster landed hard on its back. It rolled to its side, slightly stunned. Pebbles came down on top of it. The Ceratosaurus looked up and saw the driller racing over the ledge. Forty-nine tons of metal crashed down into the predator, cracking a couple of ribs while the drill punctured the flesh above its right hip. The pain gave the beast a new surge of energy. It sprang to its feet, flipping the vehicle on its back. It saw the drill and tracks continuing to rotate. The fiend was still alive! The predator moved in to finish off its enemy, ignoring the pain in its center mass.

Kim sprinted for Sakai, who guided her back to the carrier. As soon as she entered, Ward proceeded to crank the lever, lifting the ramp. The Staff Sergeant got in the passenger seat.

"Floor it," he told Morgan.

"Which way?"

"Follow it straight ahead and turn right. That'll take us north," Sakai answered. She gunned the accelerator, sending the vehicle soaring down the small hill into the trees. He glanced back through the panel. "Dr. Saldivar, we might need a little guidance." She moved up to the front row and peered through the panel.

"We'll be clear for about three miles, until we hit the marshlands. That's when we'll have to be *really* careful. One wrong turn and we'll be underwater...and it's not the water we'll have to be most concerned about."

The Ceratosaurus smashed the platform's underbelly until there was a gaping cavity in its center. The pressure sandwiched the cab between the platform and rock earth. The metal frames exploded outward. The dinosaur raked its feet and rammed its huge snout downwards, splitting the tracks. With one final blow, the engine died. The evil drill ceased to rotate, and the growls of its motor dissolved into silence. The Ceratosaurus roared into the sky. It had won.

But it heard another rumbling sound. It turned to its right, seeing another strange organism retreating into the trees. Whatever it was, it appeared to be made of a similar inedible material as the foe it had just destroyed. However, in its twisted, radiation-burned brain, it wasn't simply a matter of sustenance: it was a need to kill and reign supreme in the jungle. The creatures inside, no matter how small, attempted to challenge it. And the Ceratosaurus would die before failing to meet the challenge. It turned and galloped after the vehicle, its feet sending bits of rock hurling upwards.

"Sarge?!" It was Ward's voice. Sakai heard the thundering footsteps. He watched the mirror.

"Oh, shit," he muttered.

CHAPTER 19

Morgan fought against the instinct to wince as she drove past the onslaught of forest. They passed over huge patches of uneven terrain, wreaking havoc on each occupant inside the vehicle. She could hear Ward grunting each time he was shifted back and forth, and Vance's pained cries as the turbulence assaulted his frail body.

The Ceratosaurus was not too far behind them. Luckily, it too had difficulty navigating the forest at high speeds. Going straight on, it was easily able to keep pace. However, it had to keep diverting its direction, having learned from crashing into numerous trees already.

However, the beast was always within sight. During the chase so far were only two brief instances where they thought they had lost it. Both glimmers of hope were quickly extinguished when the dinosaur seemingly appeared out of thin air, jaws wide open, ready to snatch each occupant up.

Morgan kept her eyes fixed on the path ahead. If she looked away, even for a millisecond, she would find herself on collision course with something. Anything. The forest was a series of traps, which forced the marine to maintain a pace of half-speed. Going any faster would make it impossible to navigate.

Sakai watched the beast zigzagging behind them.

"Son of a bitch is not gonna give up," he said. "No way we're gonna get past the marshlands with him on our tail."

"We can't fight it," Ward said. "Bullets can't hurt it, and Calloway had our only rocket launcher. Even grenades barely do anything. I feel like I'm in a goddamn Japanese monster movie!"

"Grenades might not kill it, but they do cause it pain," Sakai said. "We might be able to slow it down."

"These windows won't open," Kim said.

"That's where breaking glass comes in handy," Ward said. He smashed the butt of his rifle against one of the back windows, splitting the glass out into the world behind them. He jutted his weapon through the empty panel and aimed. The creature wouldn't move in a straight direction, making a precise shot difficult. "Come on, run straight," he muttered.

The beast veered to the left, rearing up to avoid slapping its face into a tree trunk. Ward fired his under-barrel grenade-launcher, then cursed. It was as if the tree had dived in the way deliberately. The explosion launched fragments from its trunk, doing nothing against the Ceratosaurus besides aggravating its temper.

"Awe, hell," Ward muttered. He took aim and gently applied pressure on the trigger. Morgan gasped and veered right, barely avoiding a thick patch of brush. Ward's grenade soared way off into the distance, exploding deep in the forest. He groaned loudly and prepped his third and final grenade.

The carrier shook as it rolled over a layer of solid granite. He looked at the ground. The path had taken them over some kind of rocky terrain, one that was way uglier than the one they had recently escaped from. The rocks were pointed like little spikes, as if designed to prevent heavy vehicles from passing through.

He had no sooner seen the spiked ground when one of the tires ruptured. The carrier veered to the left. Morgan had no choice but to ease on the brake and steer their way out into safer ground. The rocky ground did little to slow the Ceratosaurus. It roared, then doubled its pace. It closed the distance inside of a couple of seconds. Turning its head to the side, it slashed its horn like an axe, striking the back of the vehicle.

The carrier spun as though on ice, its side slamming hard against a tree. The Ceratosaurus was victorious. It had won the pursuit. Now, it was ready to break open that shell and feast on the little creatures inside.

All Morgan saw was a blur. Her head clunked against the window during the crash, disorienting her. She heard gunfire close by. Her vision cleared and she saw Sakai sticking his gun out the window, blasting at the oncoming beast. It flinched mildly as the bullets stung its neck and chin, but didn't slow. Sakai jutted the weapon out further and aimed the grenade launcher.

The creature snarled, its eyes fixed on the weapon. With lightning speed, it spun on its heel and thrashed its tail, striking the engine hood.

The carrier was knocked several feet backward. Sakai's final grenade was fired wide.

"Damn it!" he shouted. It hurled beyond the range of sight and exploded. It was his last grenade. Ward was down to his last, and Vance and Janet had lost theirs during the cave-in.

The Ceratosaurus peered through the cracked windshield, its jawline appearing like a devilish grin. Sakai drew a breath and glanced at the group.

"Be ready to run!" He took his hand grenades off his vest and prepared to pull the pins. If he was going to be eaten, he would see to it the creature got more than a stomachache.

An angry howl filled the air. The Ceratosaurus reared back, then turned its head back and forth. Huge footsteps echoed and another howl swept the forest. The predator turned around. There was something coming. Something large.

Kim, Ward, and Janet peered through the cracked side windows. They saw the horned crest. Soon the beak-like snout came into view. Legs like tree trunks carried the dinosaur's enormous mass toward the sound of mayhem.

"The sticky-saurus," Ward exclaimed.

"*Styracosaurus,*" Janet corrected him.

"Whatever it's called, it's pissed off," he said. There were signs of burns on its upper shoulder, as well as some scarring on its crest that they hadn't seen before. Sakai's grenade had landed right beside it, awakening it from a slumber. Now, it moved at a brisk pace. It wasn't simply lumbering along, mindlessly grazing. It approached with a mission, looking for something to take its revenge on.

It saw the Ceratosaurus. Millions of years of stasis and evolution would not dispel the hatred these natural enemies had for each other. It was a war they were destined to have, whether they awakened forty-five million years ago, or forty-five million years later.

The Ceratosaurus stepped away from the vehicle and roared its displeasure at the Styracosaurus' presence. The herbivore roared back, expressing a similar tone. It leaned forward and waved its horn back and forth. In books and documentaries Janet had seen, it was always thought this kind of tactic was intended to ward off predators. But seeing it in live action, she no-longer believed that to be the case. If anything, it looked like it was taunting its enemy, its own way of saying: *Bring it, motherfucker.*

The humans sat quietly. Even Sakai was hesitant to make any movements. There was a creeping fear that if they tried to make an escape, it would attract the wrath of either beast. For the moment, they watched.

Two monsters, the last of their kind, circled each other, ready to plunge its enemy into final extinction. Each had their own weapons and advantages. The Ceratosaurus had greater maneuverability. Though the Styracosaurus had skin as tough as its own, it would offer no resistance against those jagged teeth. However, it would have to get behind that rock-hard crest. And in doing so, it would have to keep from getting impaled on that enormous horn.

Saliva trickled from the Cerato's jaws. Finally, the beast roared. The endless sizing up made it grow impatient. It charged ahead. The Styraco tucked its head low and met the challenge head on. As it closed the distance, the predator veered right in an attempt to make its way to the plant-eater's vulnerable side. The Styraco, however, had pivoted. The Cerato saw the horn closing in like a spear. It reared up, keeping its belly barely out of range. The Styraco charged forward, locking the horn under the Ceratosaurus' left leg. It reared back and cocked its head up, flipping the carnivore in a catapult motion.

The predator hit the ground with a tremendous crash. Realizing its vulnerability, it rolled to its front side and began righting itself. The Styraco charged, roaring its fury.

The horn pierced the Cerato's left hip, splitting flesh and chipping bone. The Cerato let out a sharp cry, which ended abruptly as the herbivore raked its horn upward. The intent was to use the horn as a knife to slice the flesh and widen the wound, but instead, all it did was barrel-roll the predator. However, it pressed the attack, raking its horn against any part of the Cerato it could connect with. The predator screamed, its sides spilling blood. It rolled twice, ultimately ending up on its right shoulder. It raised its leg and mule-kicked the Styraco's face, catching it in the beak. No flesh was torn, but the impact drove it back just enough for the carnivore to stand upright.

The predators circled again, the predator limping heavily. Blood trickled from the left hip, the joint clearly damaged. Given time, the wound would heal. But for that to happen, it would have to survive this ordeal. The Ceratosaurus had underestimated the herbivore. It would not make the same mistake again.

"They're busy. Let's get the hell out of here," Sakai said. Morgan tried starting the ignition. The engine rotated then died. Emergency lights flashed over the dashboard. *Fuel Leak. Oil Leak. Electrical failures.*

"Come on," she muttered. She tried again. Finally, the engine came alive with a dull, racketing sound. The whole vehicle trembled. It would not get them far.

"Just a couple miles. Get us a couple miles," she whispered. She drove forward, scraping against the tree they were knocked against. The vehicle shook more intensely as it went, the blown tire grinding against the rock bed. Soon, they found soft soil, which helped a little.

Sakai looked back. The dinosaurs never even noticed their departure. Their attention was on each other, their minds consumed with a desire to kill.

The monsters circled once more, then charged at once. Within ten feet of each other, the Ceratosaurus suddenly jumped in a low arch. Its foot came down on the Styraco's nose, just beside the horn. The herbivore fell onto its right shoulder, its face pinned to the earth.

The Cerato ignored the pain in its side and hip. It knew it had the advantage. It turned its body slightly, keeping its foot pressed firmly on the Styraco's face. Now within range of the vulnerable body, it opened its jaws and brought them down on the herbivore's kicking leg. Teeth ravaged the flesh, causing the herbivore to roar in agony. Warm blood splashed the predator's tongue, spurring it further. It mashed its jaws, sinking the teeth all the way to the bone. Like a spawn of the devil itself, the Cerato cocked its head to and fro, slicing the muscle tissue further with its teeth.

The Styraco's pain doubled in an instant, causing a burst of adrenaline that caused it to roll away. Its leg ripped from the Cerato's mouth, trailing shreds of loose flesh. It righted itself and immediately stumbled. The muscles and tendons in its leg had been completely ravaged.

The Styraco was in trouble. With its leg out of commission, it could not retreat, nor could it charge its enemy at full speed. Its options were limited. It would have to rely on its defensive tactics…and hope the Ceratosaurus would make a mistake.

The carnivore stepped forward then stopped. It sniffed the air and took in the smell of fresh blood. The herbivore's leg was tucked back. It couldn't even put the slightest amount of pressure on it. The Cerato knew what to do. Taking out one more leg would render the Styraco almost immobile. It stepped to the right. The herbivore rotated, keeping its horn pointed outward. The Cerato moved the other way. Same result. The Styraco could not afford to let it past its bone crest.

Despite the hip injury, the Ceratosaurus was still spry and unpredictable. It knelt slightly, giving the impression that it was about to jump again. The Styraco simply kept the horn pointed. Air rushed from its nostrils. The pain was aggravating. A pool of blood formed under its leg. It needed to leave and find some mud to press its body into and pack the wound.

The Cerato grew impatient. It reared up, roared, then charged straight ahead. The herbivore braced for impact, packing most of its weight onto its hind legs. The Cerato closed in and was about to sidestep. The herbivore kicked its hind legs, propelling it forward in a desperate hope to skewer the meat-eater.

But the beast saw the maneuver. It dug its heels into the ground, stopping itself. The Styraco landed a few feet shy of its target. The Cerato lunged, its jaws biting down on the horn. Both titans roared, each trying to overpower the other. The meat-eater twisted its head, trying desperately to snap the horn away. But no amount of strength could break bone that rivaled the strength of a steel beam made to hold up skyscrapers.

But there was one advantage, and that was the Styraco's lack of maneuverability. It turned its head, trying to wrench the horn through the roof of the Cerato's mouth, but the jaws maintained a firm, sideways grip. Putting all of its weight behind it, the Cerato shoved itself downwards, forcing the Styraco on its weak side. Struggle shook the beasts, until finally, the herbivore fell forward.

The Cerato released the horn and lunged, its jaws clamping down on the Styraco's left shoulder. The wounded animal screamed as teeth punctured its flesh. It threw its nose at an upward angle, trying desperately to catch the biter with its horn. But the Cerato was out of reach. Worse, it stomped a foot down on its face, pinning it once again to the ground. This time, the herbivore did not have the leverage to roll away.

It kicked and thrashed, unable to free itself. The three-fingered arms went to work, slashing its belly before grabbing on to the leg. The Cerato reared up, swallowed the mouthful of blood it had taken, and plunged its jaws down again. This time, they pierced the neck, right behind the crest. The Styraco convulsed in agony. Rivers of blood streamed from its many wounds. The ligaments in its shoulder had been shredded, rendering both front legs useless. It could not run. It could not balance. It could not fight.

It didn't stop it from trying, but its efforts had been reduced to frail jolts and thrashes. The Ceratosaurus maintained its grip for several more seconds, feeling its enemy growing weak. Finally, it lifted up, rolling the Styracosaurus on its back. It moaned once more before the jaws clamped down on its throat. Teeth shredded its airway. Its lungs filled with its own blood. The Styraco kicked a couple more times, each thrust weaker than the last, until finally, the life faded from its body.

The Ceratosaurus maintained its grip for another minute. Now confident of its opponent's demise, it let go. It stood straight on its legs and roared triumphantly into the sky. It had done its ancestors proud. It was a true king of the wilderness.

Despite this, the beast wasn't fully satisfied. It still longed to kill its challengers. It turned to where it had pinned the strange 'creature' that carried the little ones. It was no longer there. It sniffed, picking up the odd trail from the black blood that leaked from its wounds.

The dead Styraco would still be there when it was ready to feed. First, the Ceratosaurus would hunt its other enemies and slaughter them.

CHAPTER 20

"Come on, baby," Morgan repeatedly said as she steered the carrier through the forest. The vehicle dragged heavily on its flat tire. She could go no faster than thirty miles per hour. That was no problem, so long as there wasn't a giant dinosaur in her rear-view mirror. So far, there were no signs of the Ceratosaurus.

The air took on a soupy quality. It was wet and mucky, and within seconds, it felt like the humidity had doubled.

"We'll want to slow down soon," Janet said. "We've got to be getting close to the marshes.

"Is that what I'm smelling?" Morgan said.

"Probably," Janet said. "There's solid ground that'll lead us through it. But we'll have to move carefully."

"Not that this thing can handle anything more," Morgan said. The group was quiet as they approached the marsh. Sakai watched their surroundings, keeping a close watch for the Ceratosaurus, and any other threat.

The plants grew darker the further they went. There were fewer trees, though the flora in-between them nearly doubled. Driving through it was a nightmare. It seemed every square inch was covered in huge wet plants.

"How the hell did these pirates drive through this?" Morgan muttered.

"They just took the long way around," Janet said. "At the time, nobody was worried about trying to outrun oversized dinosaurs."

"The good old days," Sakai mumbled. He kept his eyes on the window, watching the thick forest. He leaned forward and gripped his rifle tighter. Something had moved. He waited a moment, then suddenly, it

128

appeared again. Bird-like in shape, it ran through the jungle at lightning speed, only appearing momentarily before disappearing behind the veil of green. "Marines. Heads up. We've got raptors on our tail."

"Where?" Ward asked. He moved from window to window, watching the forest with anticipation. Kim and Chuck hugged the center, while Vance kept an eye through the broken back window of the vehicle. For a brief moment, she caught a quick glimpse of the brown reptilian poking its head out from a huge bush. Its eyes were wide and green, its mouth almost looking like a satanic grin. In the blink of an eye, it had dipped back in.

"Oh, shit. They're studying us," she said.

"What? Is this a homework assignment for them?" Ward remarked.

"They're almost smart enough to tackle such tasks," Janet said. "But to elaborate my point, they're prepping an attack. They know we're in this carrier. They see it's damaged. They're looking for a way in."

"In that case, Doc, I'd stay away from that crack in the wall," Ward said. Janet stared at the large crevice in the side of the vehicle where it had slammed against the tree. It was wide enough for a raptor to squeeze its head through.

"You make a very good point," she said.

"Right I do," Ward said. "Hate to see those pricks bust their way through—" He heard the heavy thud of something hitting the wall behind him. Sharp claws reached through the broken window and snatched him by the pack. Ward twisted, his back arching. As he turned, he saw the drooling jaws on the other side of the window.

Vance groaned loudly as she righted herself. She thrust her pistol out and fired several rounds into the reptilian's neck. It cried out and let go. The flattened tire passed over its body, crushing it and smearing it against the moist ground. Ward shot into the aisle, his hands repeatedly brushing over his body.

"Shit! Fuck!" he shouted.

"You're welcome," Vance said. All eyes went to the left side as two more raptors collided with the carrier. With bounding leaps, they landed on the hull and dug their claws onto any ledge they could find. With that side of the vehicle so crumpled up, there was plenty to hold on to.

One stuck its head through the crack and tried to widen it, slicing its own skin against the edge in the process. The weak metal creaked as the space widened. The creature turned its head as Ward stepped up to it. It roared and lunged, the jaws stopping a few inches shy. It stuck its long neck in again as far as it could go, its jaws hyperextending. Those razor teeth snapped down on the muzzle of his gun.

"I should warn you of the aftertaste," Ward said. He squeezed the trigger, blowing the back of the creature's head out through the breach. As it fell away, he turned his aim onto the other. It twisted in agony as red holes popped along its chest and neck, then fell into the grass. Several other pack members raced parallel with the carrier. The terrain was hardly an obstacle for them. Their minds were like computers, able to detect every piece of jungle in their path, while also keeping track of the target.

Their scouts had proven that attacking the main body was futile. They would have to attack the front, where the prey was most vulnerable. And in observing the humans, the raptors learned about technology. This metal 'beast' was not alive, despite the fact that it moved and made noise. It was made somehow by these humans, and the one who sat in the front was the one who brought it to life. Take out the human in the front, then the whole thing would stop moving.

Morgan tried to accelerate but the carrier could only take so much. With each passing second, she saw more raptors running alongside the vehicle. Thirty seconds ago, they were almost a hundred feet out. Now, they were twenty and closing. They were on both sides, over a dozen of them in total. Not only that, but they were outrunning the carrier.

"Shit…" Her heart was racing. "Sarge."

"Keep it going," Sakai said. He stuck his rifle out the window and fired at the pack. One was hit right above the hip, the flesh popping outward. It tucked its head and fell, its brethren ignoring it, preferring to keep chase. Sakai fired several more bursts. Finally, they veered away.

The six or so on the left were closing in. Morgan drew her pistol and fired over her left arm, unable to take any decent aim. Still, she must've hit one because she saw blood splash the edge of the window frame. Looking over at it, she became all too aware that there was no glass between her and the outside.

With a bloodthirsty roar, one of the raptors made a desperate leap, its fingers wrapping over the edge of the window frame. It stuck its head inside and snapped its jaws at Morgan's neck. Screaming, she threw herself to the side, nearly putting herself in Sakai's lap. The jaws struck nothing but air. Frustrated, the raptor pressed its upper body through the window frame.

The vehicle continued racing forward, hitting all kinds of jungle while its driver avoided the jaws of death.

Sakai turned his rifle and fired a round into the creature's forehead. Its skull was almost split perfectly down the middle, right over the jaw. Its head almost resembled a big red and brown flower with the jaws and meat flaps dangling on all sides.

Morgan resisted the urge to dry-heave and pushed the dead beast out of the window. She found her pistol and sat up, then shrieked as two raptors leapt simultaneously. They both landed on the hood and pressed their snouts to the already damaged windshield. The one on her side peered through the bullet holes, smelling the dried blood from Chuck's injury. Spurred on, it proceeded to ram its head against the glass.

There wasn't even time for Sakai to shoot them off. In his efforts to save Morgan, he had left his side vulnerable. The raptors traveling alongside his vehicle returned. Like eight-foot-long grasshoppers, they leapt onto the vehicle. Some climbed over the top and started searching for a way in, while one clung to the door and stuck its head through the window, jaws wide. Sakai had only a split-second to react. He thrust the butt of the weapon into the creature's mouth, blocking it from reaching his flesh. Biting on the rifle stock, it thrashed its head left and right, trying to shake it from Sakai's grasp.

Meanwhile, shards of glass rained down on him as the two on the hood smashed the windshield. At the same time, another made its way for Morgan's door. Despite Ward's attempt to drive them away with repelling fire, the creatures were all converging on the carrier.

Glass spilled all over Morgan's lap. There was nothing between her and the beasts now. The one in front of her bared teeth and reared back, a moment from striking. She spun the wheel sharply to the right, throwing both raptors off balance. It grabbed whatever it could and held on, while its companion lost its grip and was thrown off. The remaining raptor righted itself. It looked directly at Morgan, then growled. The trick would not work a second time. It coiled its neck, then sprang.

A wall of water swept it off the carrier. It was as though the ground was yanked from under the vehicle like a rug, plunging it into a huge body of water. Those up top were thrown clear into the water. The raptor battling Sakai had lost its grip, and fell away. It threw its arms and legs wildly, unaccustomed to swimming.

While driving blindly, Morgan had driven them straight into the marsh. Algae-filled water spilled into the vehicle in huge waterfalls.

"Everybody out!" Sakai said. He pulled himself through the windshield and stood on the hood. Even standing upright, he was still ankle deep. He took a brief analysis of the situation. The carrier was sinking fast. The rear of the vehicle was high like the bow of a sinking ship. Behind it was the shore. From what he observed, this side of the marsh appeared to be a sudden drop-off.

Sakai reached down and pulled Morgan free. They stood on the hood, the water now creeping up their shins. The raptors looked like enormous rats in the water, converging on the carrier. Only now, they were searching for something to keep them afloat.

Something splashed behind them. The marines turned and saw the aftermath of a splash. Ripples traveled far out into the murky water. Near it were two other raptors swimming toward them. One of them let out a horrific howl, then arched backward momentarily before being pulled beneath the waves. A few moments passed and the other one was grabbed from below.

The water turned red as strips of flesh popped up along the surface.

"What the—" Morgan said.

"Let's not stay here and find out what's doing that," Sakai said.

Inside, Ward was cranking the lever as fast as he could, trying to get the ramp down. "Fucking…age…of…electronics," he groaned. Water was rushing in all around him. The ramp opened three feet, then suddenly it jammed against something. "Great. Just great."

"Hang on!" Sakai called from up top. He and Morgan ran across the carrier, knelt down along the back edge, and reached down. "We'll pull you up." Ward guided Kim up first, then Chuck. He heard something strike the wall behind his right shoulder. He glanced back and saw two raptors fighting to squeeze their way through the breach.

"Come on, Vance. You're next," Janet said.

"No, Doc. You go," Vance said. She was hunched forward, the water up to her chest. Her shoulder was badly smashed. The fact that she had pushed this far seemed practically superhuman. With no time to argue, Janet went to the door. Ward boosted her up into Sakai's grasp.

Metal screeched. One of the raptors had its head inside entirely. Vance pointed her pistol and fired. The first shot went wide. The next struck its left shoulder, the pain spurring the creature on.

Suddenly, the water surged in faster. It was as though something had grabbed the engine and was pulling the vehicle in deeper. Now, the water was almost up to the ceiling.

"Get out of here!" Vance said, her face barely above the surface.

"Vance!" Ward said. She fired her last shots. There was a loud metallic squeak, and the raptor pried itself inside the carrier.

"Ward, come on! We've got to go!" Sakai yelled. Ward threw his arms up and let his commander haul him up. Morgan and the civilians had already made the leap to shore.

Gunfire echoed below as Vance fought with the reptile. *Let her go out with a fight*, they each thought. They made the leap for shore, splashing down just a few feet from the edge. Those already there helped pull them up.

The carrier disappeared below the surface. Inside, Vance fired her last bullet into the intruder. Able to hold its breath, it ignored the pain and closed in. Out of bullets, Vance drew her knife and engaged the enemy in hand-to-hand underwater combat.

The water muffled her scream as a claw ripped across her abdomen. *Choke on me, you fuck!* She stabbed wildly with her one functioning arm. The blade sliced its arm and neck. The raptor drew its head back and identified the weapon. Vance went for a wide slice, but the reptile intercepted her attack. Jaws clamped down on her wrist, the talon fingers slicing surgically at the skin and muscle. With a sharp twist, the limb snapped off at the elbow, the remaining flesh stretching to its limits.

Defenseless, Vance could do nothing but gag in excruciating pain as the beast ripped mouthfuls of entrails out, turning the water around them dark red. Enthralled by the act of killing, the raptor proceeded ripping and tearing, unaware that its brethren had been dragged beneath the water's surface, and that the very thing that had killed them was actively cracking through the carrier's hull. Only with the sensation of pain did it realize something was wrong.

The group stumbled back in amazement as a fountain of water shot upward. Rotating in a grotesque funnel-shape it resembled a waterspout in the brief instance before the water fell away. The water rained down, revealing the creature it had obscured.

"Christ alive!" Chuck shouted. Towering like an enormous python was a seventy-foot centipede. Struggling in its huge pincer-like jaws was the raptor. Its tail and limbs slowed to a stop. The venom only needed a few seconds to course through its bloodstream.

Mandibles protruding from big brown palps proceeded to mash the dinosaur in its jaws. Its segmented body folded, splashing its many legs into the water. Each segment contained leg on each side, and from what the group could see, it had at least forty legs—above water so far. Two enormous antennae stretched ten feet from its huge rounded head.

"*That's* why we wanted to avoid the marshes," Janet said. Kim and Chuck were already backing away.

"You guys can stand here all day if you want to…" Kim said.

"Go! Run!" Sakai said. Janet took the lead, guiding the group along the shore. They ran through a quarter-mile of jungle until they found a stretch of dry land that led north. "This way! The camp should be less than a mile ahead."

The group carefully avoided the water's edge as they ran. There were no raptors in sight. Mostly likely, any that fell off the vehicle before it hit the water had fled as soon as the centipede appeared.

Ward looked back and saw the huge centipede chewing the dead raptor into mulch. Luckily for them, it didn't seem interested in the humans. It continued feasting until the raptor disappeared, then finally, it sank back into the lake.

"You sure that thing wasn't created by your uranium?" Ward said.

"Nope. Just a homegrown monster," Janet replied.

"Great. First dinosaurs, now fucking BUGS!" Ward said. "When we get back, I'm surface spraying the whole cruiser!"

CHAPTER 21

Camp D. At least, it was what the pirates called it. The word Sakai thought more preferable was 'junkyard'. There was scrap metal all over the place. Remnants of machinery stolen from every corner of the galaxy was being stored here.

The path from the marshlands went uphill, eventually leading to a vast open area with few trees. There were a series of tall rock formations to the north connecting to the valley where Sakai and Morgan had first encountered the raptors. When the team arrived at the camp, their clothes had mostly dried, though the stench of the swamp still clung to them.

Kim and Chuck both fell to their knees. Despite their exhaustion, they were both smiling ear-to-ear at the sight of a Milburn-Class shuttle.

"Oh, please tell me that thing still works," the young man said. Getting off this planet was more imperative than ever. Not only would the pain be returning soon, but there was no telling how many bacterial microbes seeped into his wound. He would have to be placed in a cryo-bed to prevent any infection from spreading.

"We're going to find that out right now," Sakai said. Even the Staff Sergeant couldn't disguise the exhaustion in his voice. They quickly swept through the camp. Like the rest of the pirate gang, this camp had been ambushed, likely by raptors. There was definitely a skirmish of some kind. There were motorcycles turned over. One of the Jeeps had plowed into a tree in an attempt to retreat; one of the other shuttles had crashed a few hundred yards to the northeast, its ruins spread across the valley. By the looks of it, they attempted an escape, only to be ambushed by the pterodactyls.

"Well, I think we can say there's no pirates," Ward said. The group converged on the shuttle.

The Milburn-Class shuttle was typically used as a personnel carrier by the mining colonies of Rotank, taking works on and off planet between shifts. Its originally silver hull had turned red from repeated exposure to the maroon colored spice surface. Judging by the drums of cleaning solution stored outside, these pirates were hoping to give the ship a decent cleansing before selling it on the black market.

Sakai approached the fuselage door and opened the control panel. He pressed the button to open the door. There was a dull 'clunking' sound, followed by that of rust trickling to the ground. The ramp opened up, knocking off flakes of rust from the edges.

The inside of the vehicle was a mixture of red and grey, a result of the residue caking into the fabric after falling from the miners' outfits after completing their shifts on Rotank.

Sakai and Ward stepped into the empty vessel and moved up into the cockpit. Ward sat in the pilot's seat and immediately began inspecting the controls. The entire console was covered in all kinds of dust, making it difficult to read the labels.

"Please tell me you can fly us out of here in this thing," Sakai said. Ward found the starter and pressed it. Both men smiled as the engines began powering up.

"Staff Sergeant, I can officially tell you that I can fly us out in this thing," Ward laughed. At that moment, the engines died, along with Ward's smile. "Well—that was anticlimactic."

"What's wrong with it?" Sakai asked.

"Computer's still running. Let me run a diagnostic." Ward tapped several keys into the computer system. The screen flashed into a series of blueprints, displaying the entire ship. A marker then flashed on the starboard engine. Ward zoomed in. "Okay, nothing to panic about. The engine's just flooded with a shit ton of residue. The pirates were probably gonna clean this thing out, then sell it off as though it was new. They just haven't gotten around to doing it before they became raptor chow."

"I saw the barrels of cleansing fluid and the machinery. They've practically set it up for us," Sakai said.

"At least they've done something useful," Ward chuckled. They walked outside, where the rest of the group anxiously awaited.

"What's the word?" Janet asked.

"We'll be leaving shortly. We just need to get the soot out of the starboard engine," Sakai said. "Relax as best you can. This'll take roughly fifteen minutes or so."

"I can help," Chuck offered. He started getting up, only for Kim to push him back down.

"No," Kim said. "You rest."

"She's right," Sakai said. "Just bear with us. We'll have you off the planet in no time." The marines proceeded to move the drums of cleaner toward the pump. Ward unscrewed a cap from the engine and firmly attached the hose, while Morgan removed several panels to allow the dirty fluid to wash out. She then helped Sakai lift the drum to fill the pump. "Alright, that's enough," Sakai said.

"Alright, I gotta try starting the engines again," Ward said.

"Okay. Let me know when to start the pump," Sakai said. He looked at Morgan. "You did well, Marine. Go and stand watch while we finish this up." Morgan nodded. His voice no longer carried the disdain it had when the team first arrived. There was a true sense of respect and belonging for a marine that had proven her worth.

Morgan walked back to the civilians and watched the forest. A wave of optimism swept through the group. They were at the end of this horrible journey, just minutes away from getting back on board the cruiser. There was also a sense of loss. It was hard not to notice the missing presence from Dr. Fry and the fallen marines.

Kim's hands were still shaky from the morning's events. She had witnessed Martin get eaten, an image that would flash in her mind as long as she lived. Chuck's hands came over hers.

"You saved our asses back there," he said to her.

"Dr. Fry saved our asses," she said. "He led the thing away from me."

"Well, thanks to him, and your quick thinking, you'll get to see your son again," Chuck said. Kim smiled. Thinking of her boy always resulted in a smile.

"Yes," she said. She wiped a tear away then looked at Chuck. "Would you like to meet him?" Chuck laughed.

"Tell you what: How 'bout we get to know each other a little better, then down the line, he and I can get acquainted? What are your thoughts?" Kim answered by pressing her lips to his, something that caught Chuck off guard, but he did not protest against. After a minute, Kim broke away, still holding his face in her hands. "I suppose you approve of that idea." They shared a laugh and hugged each other.

Kim looked over at Morgan. "Don't forget our bet when we get on board your ship."

"I haven't forgotten," Morgan said.

"Your boy's message is probably waiting for you right now," Chuck added. Morgan faked a smile, then looked away. It seemed too good to be true. She felt her stomach tightening up again, and the flood of self-doubt came racing back. Janet placed a hand on her shoulder. They looked each other in the eye. Somehow, even though Morgan never explained to anyone her criminal background, Janet could sense it.

"I'm proud of you, Private Bordales," she said. "You're doing the right thing. Don't let anyone tell you different. And also, thank you for getting us out of this mess."

Morgan nodded in appreciation. "Thank you."

A tremor passed beneath their feet. From deep in the forest came deep rumblings. Like drumbeats, they grew intensely louder. Finally, an evil roar echoed out of the forest, scaring several birds from the canopy.

"That damn Ceratosaurus followed us all the way up here," Janet said.

"How did it get past the swamp?" Kim asked.

"Same way we did," Morgan said. Sakai could hear it too. He was still running the cleaner through the pump.

"Ward, what's the soonest we can wrap this up?"

"We still gotta get more of the crap out of the engine or it'll stall," Ward said. "Five minutes at the earliest."

"We might not have five minutes," Sakai said, listening to the thumps growing nearer. He grabbed up his rifle and aimed into the woods. "Janet. Kim. Chuck, move on back."

"Should we get in the ship?" Kim asked.

"That thing will crack the hull like an egg," Sakai said. "Hide behind that junkpile. Keep out of sight." The civilians hurried behind the rubble and crouched low. Their breathing grew shaky.

Sakai approached the tree line. "Get back, Marine."

Morgan backtracked toward the shuttle. She could feel her heart going haywire.

"Sarge…"

"Hold fast," Sakai said. Morgan sucked in a deep breath and forced herself to focus. Branches smashed in the distance and crashed to the earth. Trees swayed back and forth as a huge mass passed between them.

"Sarge," Morgan said. "We won't be able to hold it off. These weapons are ineffective against it."

"We have no other choice, Marine," Sakai said.

"Yes…we do, actually," Morgan muttered. She looked to her right and saw the motorcycle lying on its side. A plan sparked in her mind. "I can lead it away," she told Sakai. The Staff Sergeant shook his head initially, then stopped as reality set in. It was obvious that the predator would wade right through them effortlessly. Realizing this, he glanced at her.

"What are you thinking?" he asked. Morgan looked again at the motorcycle.

"Pit a prehistoric alpha predator with a modern-day alpha predator," she said. As she spoke, the creature broke through the tree line. It stood high and roared at the puny humans that had dared to challenge it. It thrashed its tail, shattering several tree branches like toothpicks. Its mouth and neck were bloodstained from its battle with the Styracosaurus.

Its enormous legs carried it into the camp where it set eyes on the two marines. It looked over at the ship, attracted by the humming sound of the pump.

Ward felt his bowels threatening to loosen as he watched the creature eyeball the ship with interest. He activated his commlink and hit the transmitter.

"Sarge?" he said.

"Keep that engine running," Sakai said. He backed up slowly. There was no way around it: Once the Cerato started its rampage, there would be no stopping it.

Morgan slowly stepped to the right. As she did, she noticed a limp on its left leg. Then she saw the blood trickling from the large gash in its hip, received during its battle with the Styracosaurus.

She picked up the pace with two fast steps. The creature turned its head, fixed its eyes on her, then roared.

"GO!" Sakai shouted.

Morgan ran as fast as she could. Her life flashed before her eyes as thundering footsteps smashed down behind her. She reached the bike, straightened it, and started the engine.

Sakai blasted his rifle, striking the beast along its back. It flinched slightly, disturbed by the sting of the bullets peppering its skin, but didn't slow in its attempt to catch its prey.

The Sergeant pulled a grenade from his armor, yanked the pin, then hurled it at the creature's head. It bounced off its neck, fell along its side, and detonated. The sudden force caused the creature to stagger to its left, then stumble from its injured hip.

The bike engine roared. Morgan shouldered her rifle and fired several bursts into the carnivore's face. It shook its head then snapped its jaws, visibly irritated.

"Come on, *Barney,* you want dinner? I'll take you to a whole buffet!" She accelerated the bike into the woods, blazing past the Cerato's snapping jaws. Roaring angrily, it raced into the forest after her.

Sakai dove to the ground, avoiding its whip-like tail swinging over him as the beast turned. Roaring its displeasure, it charged into the woods after the marine.

"Get in the ship!" Sakai yelled to the civilians. They dashed from the junkpile and boarded the ship.

"What about Morgan?" Janet asked. Ward hurried into the cabin and looked out into the forest. The Cerato's crashing footsteps echoed as it pursued his teammate.

"We can't leave her behind, Sarge," he said. Sakai inhaled deeply and weighed his options. Chasing after Morgan would be futile, as he needed to remain with the ship to protect it against other predators. At the same time, he couldn't leave Morgan behind, especially after witnessing her risk her life to draw the creature away from the ship. Then again, going after the creature could risk drawing it back here where he didn't want it.

"Sergeant?" Janet said. Sakai pulled his pack off and opened it, exposing the fast rope inside.

"Ward, you think you can keep this ship level over the trees?"

"If the engines cooperate, I can do it," Ward said.

"Good. I've got an idea. But first, let's hurry up and test this engine out again!"

CHAPTER 22

The wind assaulted Morgan's face. Her heart jolted with each footstep the Cerato made. She could almost feel its hot breath on her neck, even though it was thirty feet behind her.

She had to keep herself from gaining too much distance. If the creature deemed her too difficult to catch, it would give up and return to the ship. Of course, she couldn't let it get too close either. Even with its injury, the Ceratosaurus proved it was capable of great bursts of speed.

It roared angrily, its head smashing through thick clusters of branches. Each impact generated a shockwave that made Morgan's heart flutter. She squinted through the barrage of wind. She was going downhill, twice as fast as she anticipated. The bike was easier to maneuver than the carrier, but the terrain was still just as unruly as ever.

She glanced back momentarily and saw she was still roughly thirty feet ahead of the Cerato. Its huge, bulky head was covered in red marks from the endless assault on the trees. Despite the cost, it did not want to lose its prize.

Morgan looked back. "SHIT!" She swerved to the left to avoid the enormous rock directly ahead. As she swerved, she hit a bump in the ground, causing her to go airborne for several feet. Gritting teeth, she landed, swerving back and forth to keep her balance. She then realized she was moments away from smashing directly into a tree. She swerved to the right, missing it by a narrow margin. She could feel the bike wobbling back and forth. The only way to regain control was to slow down. The earthshattering footsteps several meters back reminded her that this would be something she'd want to accomplish quickly.

She applied the brake, slowing herself nearly to a stop, then quickly regained her balance. The Cerato let out a deafening roar. Ignoring the pain in its leg, it sprinted for the target. Morgan saw its shadow encompass her whole body. The creature was over her now, jaws open wide like a Venus fly trap. She let out a scream and gunned the accelerator. The bike carried her forward. She had no sooner moved when those jaws smashed down behind her, scooping up nothing but earth.

It took off in a sprint, leaning heavily on its left side. It leaned forward to snatch the fleshy being off the strange apparatus that carried it away from it. This time, Morgan literally could feel its hot breath on her back. She veered left, which nearly took her into another tree, forcing her to weave around it.

Once again, the wind assaulted her face. This time, it came with a thick, musty smell. She noticed the moisture building up on the plant-life around her. She was almost at the marshes.

She kept going. She HAD to keep going. She was so close now… Racing ahead, she entered a large wet area with fewer trees. Puddles of water covered the ground in front of her. Her tires sliced through those puddles, sending small curtains of water out to the sides.

Up ahead was the big lake where they had seen the enormous bug.

"Almost there…" she said to herself. Her breathing grew shaky. Each of the predator's footsteps shook her insides. Her heart fluttered so fast, she felt it would burst out any second. There were no trees around them, thus, nothing to slow the monster down.

Frustrated, in pain, and sensing this new opportunity to end the chase, the Ceratosaurus launched itself into another full-speed sprint. Without a series of branches assaulting its face, it could move in a straight line and close the distance. After several huge strides, it was on top of her. It lowered its head, turned it horizontally, and opened its jaws around the bike.

In the blink of an eye, Morgan saw teeth on each side of her. Screaming, she tilted the bike forward. The front tire hit a dip in the ground, causing the bike to flip forward over end, flinging the marine for several yards. She tucked her head inward and absorbed the landing with her shoulder.

The Cerato caught the bike in midair, shook it side to side, then smashed it to the ground like a child with a toy airplane. The bike exploded into a series of parts that bounced along the creature's feet. It continued ravaging the bike until the taste of fuel splashed its tongue. It dropped the remains and spat, shaking its head repeatedly. Finally, after ridding itself of the horrid taste, the beast looked ahead at its prize, who had once again cleverly avoided its grasp. It licked its teeth, ready to conclude this pursuit with the taste of warm blood and mashed meat.

Morgan was on her side, covered in mud and algae. She had lost her rifle, leaving her with only her sidearm and knife. Knowing the lake was over a hundred feet away, it was clear she would not make it before getting snatched off the earth by those jaws.

Still on the ground, she stared at the dinosaur. For a moment, she felt the urge to throw in the towel and peacefully accept her fate. She had saved the others. She had fulfilled her duty as a marine. She had atoned for the wrongs in life; for her crimes against humanity and the wrongdoings against her family. It should've been enough to put anyone at peace...

Except, she wasn't at peace. Her mind became a hurricane of emotion. An inner voice screamed at her. She HADN'T done enough. There was more to do: more to live for.

Jamie. My sweet Jamie.

The smell of gas entered Morgan's nose. She lifted her head and saw the motorcycle's fuel can at the Cerato's feet. Instinct kicked her mind into high gear. She drew her pistol and pointed it, centering the can in her iron sights.

She squeezed the trigger. Three bullets, fired in quick succession, struck the cannister, the friction generating brief sparks that connected with the fuel. The fuel cannister erupted into a huge ball of fire. To the dinosaur, the explosion had come from nowhere. All it saw was a huge ball of flame singeing its leg and underbelly.

The enormous reptile staggered backward, providing Morgan the opportunity she needed. She sprang to her feet and ran to the lake as fast as she could. After a dozen huge strides, she had reached the water's edge. She fired several rounds into the water.

"Come on! Where the hell are you?" she shouted. She looked back and saw the enraged Cerato stepping through the wall of smoke. It saw her and began to charge. She had seconds left. Morgan grabbed her grenades, yanked the pins, and tossed them into the water. They struck down a hundred feet in and detonated, sending large waves stretching above the murky surface.

The water splashed down. Silence took over, aside from the Cerato's footprints. For a moment, it looked as though Morgan's efforts had failed.

Suddenly, the water began to spiral. Sludgy water splashed her waist and boots. In less than a moment, the lake turned into a chaotic whirlpool. That spiral then exploded high into the sky, the wave splitting apart into millions of individual droplets, unveiling the enormous centipede monster that lived beneath it.

The Cerato halted as soon as it saw the giant arthropod. It twisted its body, its antennae waving up and down, detecting signs of movement on the nearby land. It saw the prehistoric reptile and reacted by spreading its many legs wide. Its mandibles extended outward like scissor blades and let out a blaring hiss that made the dinosaur step back momentarily. The tactic had worked. The creature had struck fear into its opponent, who, in its youth and inexperience, had never encountered a being such as the centipede. The Cerato roared in an attempt to influence a similar effect on the centipede by instilling fear into it. The problem was the centipede could not experience fear. It only had instinct and a drive to survive. And to survive, it needed sustenance, rest, and a watery habitat. Having grown so long over its many decades of life, adequate sustenance was difficult to come by. Until now. A creature as large as the Cerato would sustain it for weeks. It could simply rest in its marsh and feed at its leisure.

The Cerato roared again. But the centipede didn't react, at least, not in the way the Cerato intended. It lifted its round head high above the water, matching the dinosaur's height. Much of its mass remained submerged. The dinosaur waved its horn left and right. Despite the unfamiliarity of this new foe, it still felt emboldened from its victory with the Styracosaurus. It didn't expect to face a new challenger of this size so soon, and not one so intimidating. But two alpha predators could not exist in the same terrain, now that they knew of the other's existence. There was only enough room on this town...for one.

Morgan was now standing between two titans, whose gazes were locked in a tense standoff. Conflict was inevitable: that was the plan. What wasn't part of the plan was being between them when it started.

She ran as fast as she could along the shore. Her movements attracted the attention of the Ceratosaurus. The instinct to kill took over. It turned and lunged, jaws extended.

The aggressive movement triggered the centipede's attack. Its lower half, which was coiled under the water, straightened in the span of a millisecond, launching the creature like a spring. Its head struck the Cerato's neck, driving it down on its left shoulder. Legs kicked and its multi-segmented body thrashed like a snake. The Cerato rolled, roaring angrily, while pedaling its arms and legs. It snapped its jaws downward, clamping down on the segment of the centipede's body just behind its head. It completed its roll and came up on its feet.

Morgan continued running, while hearing the sounds of chaos taking place behind her.

The Cerato held tight. Despite its bite force of thirteen-thousand pounds per square-inch, it still struggled to breach the centipede's thick exoskeleton. The pincer-like mandibles snapped, unable to reach their target and inject their deadly venom. Still, it continued snapping, desperate to pierce its enemy's flesh.

Its lower half coiled around the Cerato's body like a python. The carnivore, still keeping its jaws clamped tight near the centipede's head, felt the sting of over sixty pointed legs prodding along its hip and back.

The Cerato swung its whole body, thrashing its tail, trying to pry itself from the centipede's grasp. All it did, however, was simply spin the arthropod around with itself.

The legs near the centipede's anal segment walked it backwards, wrapping its long body over the Cerato's. Now tightly wrapped, the legs proceeded to jab into its thick skin.

The Ceratosaurus panicked. With its jaws still clamped over the arthropod, it stumbled backward.

Morgan felt the tremors of its footsteps growing stronger. She turned and saw that the beast was coming her way. Its huge tail swung horizontally, striking the branch of a nearby tree. Debris rained around her, splashing the water. Morgan threw her arms over her eyes to protect her face, then ran as fast as she could. Peering through the space between her arms, she moved away from the shore. She knew it was best to keep out of the water if possible. There was no telling what else could be waiting for her in there.

The stomping continued. Morgan looked back and saw that the dinosaur had now turned, and its tail was swinging low…its tip thirty feet from her head and closing. There was no time to think. Morgan dove to the ground, splashing mud. The tail sliced the air above her, followed by a gust of wind.

It was still coming her way, chasing her without even knowing it. Its huge feet sent tidal waves of mud splashing in all directions. Morgan gasped as it took another step back. She rolled to her left. A moment later, she felt a sheet of mud splash over her. The foot came down hard just inches from her body. The tremor literally lifted her a few inches from the ground. The Cerato continued backtracking, groaning crossly from its predicament.

It whipped its head back and forth, its jaws attempting to munch the centipede. Tiny shards of exoskeleton rained down. The Ceratosaurus continued its bite, hoping to chew the creature's head clean off. But the pain all over its body was driving it into a frenzy.

Streams of blood started running down its body. The centipede tightened its coil, compressing the Cerato's ribcage and driving its spear-like legs deeper into its flesh. The Cerato huffed and puffed. The centipede was latched on tight and would not let go. It maintained its grip, keeping the pincer jaws away from its neck, but it could feel its energy waning.

The young dinosaur regretted its decision to engage this arthropod in battle. The centipede was an older, more experienced fighter. And unlike the Cerato, it felt no sense of self-preservation beyond the need to sustain itself. It felt no pain from the bite injury behind its head. Its brain was computer-like, only detecting nerve impulses that informed it of an injury, which would heal in time.

The Cerato was in a peculiar position. For the first time in its young life, it wanted to flee. To do that, it would have to release those jaws, and doing that would accomplish nothing but provide an opportunity for the arthropod to bite it in the neck. The Cerato knew it had to keep its mouth clamped tight to keep the centipede from biting. The Cerato had no knowledge of understanding of the deadly venom, but it knew a bite from those jaws would be devastating all the same.

The Ceratosaurus grew desperate. It turned around and raced several yards uphill. It found a tree and sideswiped it with its body, trying to scrape the centipede off. All it accomplished was snapping branches and chunks of bark.

Morgan caught her breath and stood up. She was unsure where to go. The way back to the shuttle was up that hill. To get there, she would have to get around the beasts. With the way it was staggering around in every direction, she would have to risk getting stomped on to escape. Going across the lake—if she even made it that far, would put her at risk of running into any remnants of the raptor pack.

She watched as the Cerato danced, groaning incessantly from fatigue and frustration. The centipede snapped its mandibles, still unable to reach the Cerato's neck. It twisted its body, gradually prying itself from those teeth. Bits of shell rained down. The Cerato turned and slammed the bugs against the tree. The resulting shockwave sent leaves and branches crashing down. The Cerato continued pummeling the centipede against the tree, swinging its head like a baseball bat.

The centipede was hissing now. The blunt force rocked its brain. It dug its legs into the Cerato, whose sides were now covered in nearly a hundred red holes. It slammed the centipede's head again. The arthropod's movements became more frantic. It twisted its upper body, but could not get more than a few inches of movement due to the enormous bite power. To combat this problem, it would adjust its current strategy.

Its body, still wrapped around the Cerato's, scooched upward, the legs prodding its back, shoulders, and chest. The Cerato thrashed its short arms for a few short moments before they were pinned. The legs writhed, dragging the centipede's lower and middle sections up around the Cerato's neck. The legs prodded the flesh, while the body squeezed tight.

The Ceratosaurus tried sucking in a breath, but nothing got in. The body continued creeping upward. It felt several stings along the back of its head. The centipede was on the verge of constricting its face in addition to its throat.

The Ceratosaurus felt a leg prod near the corner of its left eye. A moment later, it couldn't see anything. The centipede was wrapped around its face and neck. Now, all it had to do was maintain the grip. It was just a matter of time.

The Cerato stumbled. Its nerves were on fire with the endless prodding from the legs. Also, the centipede's weight was dragging it down. It stumbled blindly, its heart racing, its lungs burning. It could feel its legs starting to buckle. All of its strength was focused on keeping the centipede from biting; a tactic that was failing it.

It thrashed its upper body, trying to slam the centipede into the tree again. In its blindness, it found nothing but air. Desperate to pry itself free, it chose a desperate maneuver. It threw itself to the ground as hard as it could, then rolled, plastering its body with mud.

Morgan swallowed hard as she saw its mass coming right towards her.

"Oh, for godsake!" she shouted. She ran out of the way, only to find herself on the shore of another lake. She could see rippling in the water, then the curving, serpent-like body of whatever dwelled inside of it. A smaller centipede? A baby? Whatever it was, it wasn't safe. She pivoted to the right, keeping just out of reach from the Cerato's tail. Its legs kicked as it completed another roll. Its plan had backfired. On the ground, the centipede had greater leverage. And now, the dinosaur was unwittingly rolling toward the water.

It let out a tired groan. Its movements began to slow. Still, it kept its jaws clamped tight, unwilling to accept defeat. It writhed, splashing up huge waves of water along the shore.

Morgan saw her chance. She was now past the monsters and had a straight shot up the hill. Hopefully, the others had waited. They had probably tried to comm her, but her receiver had been damaged. It didn't matter. She would run back. If they weren't there, she'd figure something out. Sakai was not the type to abandon people.

She made it a hundred yards when she saw movement to the right. Splashing puddles gave away the presence of something darting in the distance. Morgan paused and drew her pistol. She reloaded it with a full magazine and waited. She saw it again.

Fucking raptors! They must have regrouped at some point and made their way around the big lake. Knowing them, they were probably planning on tracking the team up to Camp D. But lucky for them, the food had foolishly come back.

The raptor stopped suddenly and gazed at her. It was several hundred feet away, with bushes and vines blocking most of its body. Morgan felt a chill. Her mind flashed to their previous tactics of deception and diversion. She turned around.

The raptor's brethren was halfway to her, ready to attack her from behind. It shrieked as it saw her turn to face it. It had the strange loud weapon pointed at it. It heard only the first crack, while simultaneously feeling the intrusive impact of the projectile on its skull.

Morgan fired two more shots, striking the raptor in the neck and lower jaw. The first shot was enough, however. The raptor's momentum sent it crashing into a forward roll. After briefly watching it go down, Morgan turned. The other was coming directly at her. She fired several shots, hitting it in the chest, ravaging its lungs. The raptor lurched, still running. Its pained screech launched drops of blood into the air. Its run slowed to a stumble and it went down.

There was more movement. Morgan caught glimpses of raptors running in the distance, circling her. They had seen their other members go down, which made them wary of their target. But she knew they were not going to let her off easy. She turned again, repeatedly catching brief glimpses of the raptors.

Morgan saw no way out. She didn't have enough bullets to fight off the pack. Hell, she was amazed she was able to take down the first two. It was inevitable they would overpower her. She would be gutted, her insides ripped out, her arms and limbs severed. The worst part: she would be alive for much of it.

She slowly turned the gun and placed the muzzle to her temple. The thought of being torn apart was almost too much. Almost. Only one thing seemed worse: the thought of quitting, even in the face of certain failure.

Morgan breathed. She turned the gun away from herself and redirected it out into the marsh. She spun on her heel and fired toward the sound of movement. The raptor had doubled back. She realized they were attempting the diversion tactic again. She spun back. Sure enough, two raptors were racing her way. She fired off several rounds. The first raptor was struck twice in the throat, causing it to barrel forward. The other took a round in the shoulder and one in the chest. It doubled over, but kept coming. Morgan squeezed the trigger. Nothing. It was at that moment she saw the slide locked back on her pistol.

She chucked the weapon, bouncing it off the raptor's snout. Its impact was hard enough to alter its trajectory, allowing Morgan to sidestep and avoid its grasp. It was fight or flight now. There was no weighing of options, only instinct, and instinct drove her to fight.

She had a second at best before it turned around.

Morgan drew her knife and leapt onto its back, wrapping her arms and legs around its body. The raptor felt the intruder and bucked, trying to shake her off. It turned its head and snapped its jaws, missing. Morgan plunged the knife into its neck. The raptor roared and stumbled. Morgan continued stabbing, sending rivers of blood into the mud. Finally, she reached as far as she could and plunged the knife directly into its throat. She twisted the blade, feeling the warmth of its blood wash over the hilt.

The raptor convulsed, then fell on its side. Morgan rolled to her feet, gasping for breath. Mud and water splashed around her. She turned. The raptors were converging. They knew she had lost the loud weapon, allowing them to take their time and close in.

There were four of them directly ahead of her, with a couple stepping out from the sides. One of them started to move in, only for another to snap at its face, driving it back. It was the leader of the pack, who wanted to take the kill for itself.

Morgan took in another breath, then raised her knife. It would be a painful death, but she would go down fighting.

Suddenly, a downdraft engulfed the pack. Water puddles rippled, and a shadow suddenly swept over Morgan. She heard the crackling of assault rifle fire. Bullets struck the lead raptor in the face, sending chunks of flesh and bone exploding on all sides.

Morgan looked up.

The rusty Milburn Shuttle hovered directly above her. Its boarding ramp was open. Standing on its edge was Sakai, held firm by a harness he had rigged. He fired down at the pack, driving them away from his marine. Bullets struck other raptors. They dispersed, confused and unnerved by the huge leviathan hovering above.

"Hold it steady," Sakai yelled to the cockpit. Ward was at the helm, carefully lowering the ship to the marsh. He avoided the few trees in the area, and maintained a watchful eye on the giant creatures battling near the lake. Sakai continued blasting the raptors until his LED blinked red. He looked back into the fuselage. Janet stood behind the entrance, fast rope in hand. The end had been tied into a loop for Morgan to hang on to. He reached out, gesturing for her to hand it to him. After tossing it to him, she fed him the slack.

"Bordales, grab the rope!" he shouted to Morgan. The fast rope landed a few feet to Morgan's right. She spun on her heel and sprinted, quickly catching the rope and slipping herself into the loop. Behind her, a raptor recovered, having been struck near the hip. It saw the human slipping into the strange tentacle. Unwilling to give up its meal, it charged.

Sakai saw the beast moving in. He took aim and fired his last burst of ammo, striking the raptor in the head. After witnessing it crash, he noticed others starting to regroup.

Morgan fastened herself into the loop and raised a thumbs-up.

"Pull up!" Sakai shouted to Ward. The pilot clutched the yoke and ascended, lifting his fellow marine high above the marsh, out of the raptors' reach. Janet and Kim proceeded to pull her up into the craft.

Morgan's feet touched metal flooring. She embraced the artificial light of the fuselage and the cycling of air. Sakai stepped in and the loading ramp closed shut. He entered the cockpit and took the seat beside Ward, while everyone in the back strapped in.

"Punch it," Sakai said.

"Don't have to tell me twice," Ward said, watching the skies for any more pterodactyls. He applied thrust, shooting the shuttle high into the atmosphere.

The Cerato rolled again, putting itself deeper into the water. Its skin had paled from lack of oxygen. It had suffered massive blood loss from its many wounds. It was alive, but the strength had left its body. Its grasp on the centipede weakened, allowing the arthropod to pry itself out. The Cerato let out a gasping roar after feeling the centipede slip out. It slashed its feet and tail, knowing how vulnerable it was. But it was pinned, defenseless. Its blindness prevented it from witnessing the centipede curl its upper half backward, angling its head toward the Cerato's exposed underside. It extended its mandibles and lunged.

The Ceratosaurus spasmed as two enormous fangs punctured its midsection. The venom poured inside and immediately went to work paralyzing the victim. The Cerato felt the centipede loosen its grasp from its neck. Yet, it still couldn't breathe. It couldn't move. It was like some invisible force was draining what was left of its energy, which didn't take long.

The Ceratosaurus lay in the mud, mouth agape, unable to move. The centipede took a hold of its ankle with its mighty pincers, then slowly backed into the water. The water rippled as it took the huge Ceratosaurus in tow. After a few minutes, both titans were submerged.

The modern predator had defeated the prehistoric.

There was no sense of glory for the centipede. Memory of the fight would quickly vanish. It had no feelings of victory or triumph. There was no ego to feed—only its stomach. The only reward that mattered in the wild forest of Malek was the satisfaction of eating your opponent.

And the centipede would feast for weeks to come.

CHAPTER 23

Sakai was the last to step out of the dock into the main passageway of the cruiser. Immediately, he felt the strange floating sensation that artificial gravity had on him. Like every other tense mission, he embraced that sensation. They were out of harm's way. The mission was complete, though at great cost. His marines had given their lives bravely and with honor, and the one team member he had the lowest hopes for had gone above and beyond the call of duty. And because of her, he was able to embrace the annoying feel of artificial gravity once more.

As he went down the passageway, he looked down at Malek's green surface. Because of their discoveries, it was likely that the planet would remain relatively untouched by human expansion. Perhaps a communications base would be established, but because of the deadly secrets discovered under the uranium bed, the United World Order would likely have to forgo deforestation. Where there was one uranium deposit, there were others, and who knows what effect they had had on the wildlife, as well as the forests themselves. The planet would remain green and thriving, the remaining dinosaurs would live out the rest of their lives, and possibly suffer the wrath of the planet's modern-day predators. Sakai had only seen a tiny fraction of the planet, but it was reasonable to assume that giant centipedes were only one member of the planet's deadly ecosystem.

He followed the group to Med Bay. Ward typed in the codes for a med-pod. A glass tube opened up. They helped Chuck remove his shirt and pants and assisted him into the pod. Janet and Ward hooked up the monitors and prepped him for cryo-sleep.

"Didn't expect you to see me like this so soon," he joked to Kim. She smiled and put a hand on his shoulder.

"I'll see you when you wake up," she said. "First, get some rest. When you wake up, a doctor will have you fixed up." She leaned down and kissed him. Ward activated the med-pod, freezing Chuck in a peaceful cryo-sleep.

The rest of the group proceeded into the briefing room.

"What happens now?" Janet asked.

"First, I got to get a message back to Headquarters," Sakai said. "Afterwards, we'll remain here and wait for reinforcements to arrive. I'm gonna have to give an in-person debriefing. After that, we'll transfer you onto a ship and send you home. We've got a couple days yet, so, simply put, we wait."

"Better here than down there," Kim said.

"Couldn't agree more," Ward replied. "I'll head into the bridge and get that transmitter ready for you, sir."

"Thanks, Marine," Sakai said. He noticed Kim and Janet sitting down. "Give me a moment to get things settled and I'll provide you with some clean clothes."

"Thank you, sir," Janet said.

"I can help with that, Staff Sergeant," Morgan said. Sakai looked at her mud-covered uniform and face. A rare smile took form over his face.

"Get yourself cleaned up first. You're a mess, Marine," he said. Morgan failed to suppress her smile. She saluted the Staff Sergeant, then did an about-face and headed for the locker rooms.

Sakai's smile remained. He would indeed be writing to the Board of Corrections and Rehabilitation. Only, it wouldn't be the letter he thought he would write. He would inform them that Morgan Bordales' debt had been paid and would advise honorary discharge at the end of her second year of service. She proved to be a good marine, but he knew it wasn't the life she wanted. It was the least he could do. He would write another letter, recommending Dr. Martin Fry for the Civilian Medal of Valor thanks to his bravery and sacrifice on Mount Dragoon.

He saw Morgan stop halfway down the corridor. To her right was the entrance to the comm room. It was clear what was going through her head. And he didn't mind. Sakai proceeded to the bridge and initiated his message to the incoming ships.

****

Morgan hesitated, fearing the likely disappointment she would feel after logging into her message board. The urge was too great. She had to check.

She entered the room and took a seat. The computer took an excruciatingly long minute to boot up. When it did, she punched in her personal ID codes. After another excruciating minute, it loaded the message board. All she had to do now was sign into her account.

She hesitated again. Why put herself through this? She remembered coming close to tears last time she did this. This time she would surely break, especially after experiencing the loss of several fellow marines.

Morgan took a deep breath. Finally, she punched in the password. The screen flashed to her message page.

Her eyes widened at the bold black letters indicating a new message. She quickly clicked on it. As she expected, she came to tears, but not for the reason she feared. She simply read the name over and over again, making sure her mind wasn't playing tricks.

"Kim?" she called out. She heard approaching footsteps. Kim poked her head inside.

"What's up?" she asked.

Morgan sniffled and wiped her eyes. She turned around, smiling ear-to-ear.

"I owe you a hundred Smiths."

THE END

CHECK OUT OTHER GREAT DINOSAUR THRILLERS

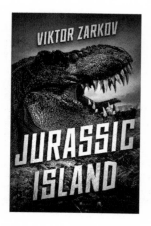

JURASSIC ISLAND
by Viktor Zarkov

Guided by satellite photos and modern technology a ragtag group of survivalists and scientists travel to an uncharted island in the remote South Indian Ocean. Things go to hell in a hurry once the team reaches the island and the massive megalodon that attacked their boats is only the beginning of their desperate fight for survival.

Nothing could have prepared billionaire explorer Joseph Thornton and washed up archaeologist Christopher "Colt" McKinnon for the terrifying prehistoric creatures that wait for them on JURASSIC ISLAND!

K-REX
by L.Z. Hunter

Deep within the Congo jungle, Circuitz Mining employs mercenaries as security for its Coltan mining site. Armed with assault rifles and decades of experience, nothing should go wrong. However, the dangers within the jungle stretch beyond venomous snakes and poisonous spiders. There is more to fear than guerrillas and vicious animals. Undetected, something lurks under the expansive treetop canopy . . .

Something ancient.

Something dangerous.

Kasai Rex!

CHECK OUT OTHER GREAT DINOSAUR THRILLERS

WRITTEN IN STONE
by David Rhodes

Charles Dawson is trapped 100 million years in the past. Trying to survive from day to day in a world of dinosaurs he devises a plan to change his fate. As he begins to write messages in the soft mud of a nearby stream, he can only hope they will be found by someone who can stop his time travel. Professor Ron Fontana and Professor Ray Taggit, scientists with opposing views, each discover the fossilized messages. While attempting to save Charles, Professor Fontana, his daughter Lauren and their friend Danny are forced to join Taggit and his group of mercenaries. Taggit does not intend to rescue Charles Dawson, but to force Dawson to travel back in time to gather samples for Taggit's fame and fortune. As the two groups jump through time they find they must work together to make it back alive as this fast-paced thriller climaxes at the very moment the age of dinosaurs is ending.

HARD TIME
by Alex Laybourne

Rookie officer Peter Malone and his heavily armed team are sent on a deadly mission to extract a dangerous criminal from a classified prison world. A Kruger Correctional facility where only the hardest, most vicious criminals are sent to fend for themselves, never to return.

But when the team come face to face with ancient beasts from a lost world, their mission is changed. The new objective: Survive.

CHECK OUT OTHER GREAT DINOSAUR THRILLERS

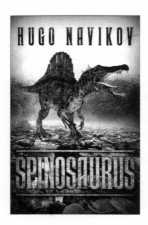

SPINOSAURUS
by Hugo Navikov

Brett Russell is a hunter of the rarest game. His targets are cryptids, animals denied by science. But they are well known by those living on the edges of civilization, where monsters attack and devour their animals and children and lay ruin to their shantytowns.

When a shadowy organization sends Brett to the Congo in search of the legendary dinosaur cryptid Kasai Rex, he will face much more than a terrifying monster from the past.

Spinosaurus is a dinosaur thriller packed with intrigue, action and giant prehistoric predators.

LAND OF DEATH
by Eric S Brown & Alex Laybourne

A group of American soldiers, fleeing an organized attack on their base camp in the Middle East, encounter a storm unlike anything they've seen before. When the storm subsides, they wake up to find themselves no longer in the desert and perhaps not even on Earth. The jungle they've been deposited in is a place ruled by prehistoric creatures long extinct. Each day is a struggle to survive as their ammo begins to run low and virtually everything they encounter, in this land they've been hurled into, is a deadly threat.